Also available from K. R. Max:

Alphas & Innocents

Billionaire Santa And His Innocent Intern
Her Dominant Professor
Her Dominant Neighbor
Her Dominant Lawman

Her Dominant Boss

Caden (Her Dominant Boss #1)

CADEN:
Her Dominant Boss #1

K. R. Max

DEDICATION

For my mother, for believing in me and
supporting me when I needed it most

ACKNOWLEDGMENTS

To Susan Bischoff, my wonderful editor, friend
and general partner in crime – you're the best.

Caden: Her Dominant Boss #1

Keeley

"Saw Jason moved out."

My heart sinks. Of all the shit I have to handle today, my landlord is top of the list of things I've been hoping to avoid. Mentioning Jason is his way of reminding me I'm alone again, with no one to help with rent or reassure me that this too shall pass. No one to comfort eat ice cream with, or ramen, since that's all I can afford. Most of all, no one to run interference between me and any passing lecherous assholes. I could have gone at least a few more hours without having to face this bunch of shitty facts, but no such luck.

Of course not. Because I have no luck at all.

I stay focused on my mailbox, turning the key, opening the door, hoping Wallis will get the message and move on. I don't need him making me feel like a failure, on top of everything else. Besides, one of these envelopes might actually hold a job offer.

I stifle the impulse to laugh. Like anything good's going to happen to me today.

As if he's determined to prove me right, I feel Wallis' hand on my hip, too low on my hip. I swallow and turn around, finding him even closer than normal.

"I know you've been out of work a while," he says. He's not even trying to be sympathetic, his eyes hot with lust as they rove down my body.

Ugh. This is why I spend as little time as possible in the public areas of this building. Wallis has always made me feel uncomfortable. It wasn't so bad when I had a job. I was hardly ever here. It wasn't even so bad when Jason, my boyf—, sorry, *ex*-boyfriend, still lived here. He was a big guy. A big douchebag, as I found out two days ago when I got home to find he'd emptied our apartment of his stuff, and most of mine, before taking the contents of my bank accounts too. Still, he'd been big enough to scare Wallis into behaving himself whenever he saw me.

But he's not here anymore. I've got no one to watch my back now. Although, if I think about it, I never did. Just guys getting close enough to stab me in it.

I shove the helplessness and anger back in their box and summon up my best 'I've got to go now' smile as I push past him. Or try to. Usually he lets me go, but this time he seems determined to make a point, and he pushes me back against the mailboxes. Fear rolls in my belly, cold and sour.

"Now, now," he says, a cruel smile curving his thin, wet lips. "We're having a conversation. Don't be rude."

"I have an interview to go to," I tell him, trying, and failing, to force some steel into my voice.

"You've got five minutes for your landlord," he tells me, leaning in closer, and I grit my teeth against the rancid stench of his breath. He lifts a finger to the skin of my chest, where my blouse dips down to show just a hint of cleavage. I'm not dressing like a ho to get a job, but it's the smartest shirt I own, and I need to show my best side to prospective employers. But the way he's touching me makes me want to pull a sack over my head. "I just want you to know, if money's tight, we can work out some kind of alternative arrangement."

The impulse to punch him is almost overwhelming. Maybe it's the knowledge that if I lose this apartment, I'll be homeless, because there's nowhere else I can go. No job, no references, not even any friends or family to crash with. I'd be screwed. I need a place to live, even one with cockroaches big enough to put a leash and collar on and take to the dog park.

Instead, I summon up a smile. I know it's weak, can tell by the malicious glee in his eyes as he registers my fear of him. There's nothing I can do about that. Usually, I find it easier to deal with this asshole. Today is not that day. Today is the day I'll count a win if I get through it without having a screaming, crying meltdown and throwing myself off a bridge.

"Thanks, Wallis. I'll bear that in mind."

He hooks his finger into my blouse, pulling it, and me, towards him. I can't resist. I can't afford to piss him off. He runs this building. I have no idea how he managed to afford it in the first place, but he did, and now he gets to take advantage of any tenant unfortunate enough to be in a tight spot financially. I also can't afford to damage this shirt. I don't have money for another one, and damn him, he knows it.

He leans in, staring into my eyes, no doubt getting off on my fear, my helpless anger. If I don't get a job soon, I'm going to find out what else he gets off on, and I know I won't enjoy a single second of it.

Damn it. I *need* a job.

***

Caden

I step out of the diner, sipping my coffee and trying not to smirk at Parker, my driver, as he glares at anyone within a twenty foot radius while standing next to my town car, idling by the crumbling curb. He hates that I insist on coming to this place, only half a block shy of the ghetto, every morning for coffee. Always reminds me how he's supposed to be my bodyguard, not a spectator at the scene of my death.

I always remind him that money can't buy everything. I may be a billionaire, but I can't move an entire diner to a decent part of town. Believe me, I've looked into it. The cost was prohibitive, even by my standards.

I have suggested to Parker that I drive myself if the area upsets him that much. The only response he gave that idea was a look that my mother must have felt ninety miles away in the Hamptons, because she called later that same day to see how I was, an occurrence unusual enough to warrant a note in my calendar.

That said, I don't dawdle. I love my coffee, but I'm not willing to die for it, and people around here are desperate to do just about anything for a quick buck, even with two hundred and fifty pounds of Parker looking on. It doesn't pay to hang around and tempt fate.

I'm only a couple of feet from the car when a blur of motion has me turning to look, but not before someone runs straight into me, bouncing off with a breathless "Oof!". I reach out to catch them on instinct, my arm wrapping around the stranger before they can hit the pavement.

Immediately, my brain short circuits, my mind purely focused on the soft weight of warm flesh in my arms. Firm breasts press against my chest as it registers that I'm holding a woman, and a beautiful one at that.

Her makeup is basic, not enough to hide the natural beauty of high cheekbones, flawless skin, and large hazel eyes, fringed with dark honey eyelashes. Her lips are soft and full, like the rest of her, and as I stare at her mouth, I can't help wondering what it would feel like wrapped around my cock. The thought sends a rush of heat to my groin, my cock hardening immediately to the point of pain. She clearly feels it too, because that warm skin turns rosy over her cheekbones and her lips part to form an O. Her breath comes short and so does mine.

"Sir? You okay?"

Parker's deep voice, dark as a mineshaft, jerks

me back to the real world. I drag my eyes away from the woman in my arms to nod at him.

"Yes. Are you okay?" I ask the luscious armful of female currently pressed up against me.

The feel of her body so close to mine is nothing new, in itself. I've been blessed with good genes, and that combined with my net worth means I'm never short of female company, should I wish it.

Lately, though, I haven't been in the mood. They're always after something, usually a wedding ring, or at least an unlimited allowance. I didn't get where I am by lacking in discernment. It's been months since I even took a date to any of the various events I have to attend. It's simply less hassle that way. No matter how clear I am with my various companions regarding the temporary nature of our liaison, I always end up having to block yet another telephone number from my phone when they harass me for days after, wanting to know what they did wrong and how they can make it up to me.

The fact of the matter is, it's been a long time since I reacted to anyone with the intensity I'm currently feeling. I don't see the point of maintaining a relationship when I have lost interest. That said, I can barely construct a coherent thought right now as the woman I'm currently holding wriggles against me, except to register that it feels good.

Maybe too good.

We are in public, after all. As I look around, a skinny guy with lank hair looks away. Like he's avoiding my gaze.

"You can let go of me now," she says, and I

blink, then stare at her. Her face is flushed, and a pulse hammers at the base of her throat. She's breathing in choppy gasps, her chest heaving as she pants for air. I recognize all these signs, but there's one thing which isn't adding up the same way.

Now that I focus properly on her, I notice she's not undulating in that sensual manner women use to let me know they're ready and willing to do a whole lot more than stand in a drafty ballroom, eating canapes and making small talk.

She's actually trying to get away from me.

I think back, but no. I honestly can't remember the last time this happened.

I'm so shocked, I let go, and she shoots out of my arms as though spring-loaded. The skinny guy on the corner straightens, and a protective instinct I didn't even know I had roars to life within me. I don't even think twice before my hand whips out to wrap around hers. I can't let her leave yet. I just can't. I turn and drag her into the back of the town car, and Parker immediately slams the door shut behind us.

Keeley

I have no idea what just happened. One minute I was running along the sidewalk, hoping to catch the 29 bus downtown so I could pound pavement and rustle up some more interviews, the next I was bouncing off a guy so built, he should have been wearing a roof, not a suit which cost more than a year's rent.

I may be permanently skating the underside of

poverty, but I've worked in enough corporate offices to know what rich looks like, and it looks like I just knocked its coffee on the ground.

Great.

He didn't seem bothered at the time, but now I'm sprawled across the back seat of his car. His grip around my wrist doesn't lessen, and before I can even scream, the door closes behind us. Two seconds later, the car pulls away from the curb, and I'm left in the dark with a guy who seems infinitely more dangerous than Wallis. And yet, I'm not screaming for help.

I stare up at him, trying, and failing, to catch my breath. The man is just gorgeous. A hard face above broad shoulders, framed with inky black hair styled so neatly that I want to mess it up, maybe run my hands through it while bouncing up and down in his lap…

Fuck me, where had that thought come from? After all, I'm a virgin. But something about this guy has me thinking thoughts I shouldn't be having.

My face burns. I try to look away, but his gaze has me trapped. Deep blue eyes, framed with long black eyelashes, bore into me, and I'm horrified to feel my pussy tingling with heat, moisture dampening my panties as my nipples harden to aching points.

Well, I *should* be horrified.

But I'm not really. I'm…horny. I want this man. Two days after the last one left me almost bankrupt and liable for rent in a building with a real dick of a landlord, I should be thinking about all the ways this is a really terrible idea. Instead, my skin is prickling with awareness. I'm deeply aware of the burn of his skin against my wrist, the heat settling into my bones, winding through my blood to pool in my belly. My mouth is dry and when I lick my lips, his eyes follow the motion, darkening with an intent which should have me running, or at least pushing away from him, but instead, I'm crawling closer.

He draws me against him, his free hand skimming over my shoulder and down my back to curve under my ass, lifting me into his lap so that I'm straddling him.

"Sorry about that," he mutters. "There was a man, looking very suspicious...Are you okay?"

My skirt rides up, and he pulls me closer, the bulge in his pants pressing against my clit as he settles me tight against him. I gasp, "Yes," as sensation skitters through me.

"Where did you come from?" he murmurs, brushing a strand of hair off my face. He slides his hand around the back of my neck and pulls me closer. With a fraction of an inch between our mouths, I moan, unable to speak, desperate to feel his lips on mine.

I sway into him, my lips meeting his as my nipples rub against his chest, and I moan again. He takes advantage of my parted lips to sweep his tongue into my mouth, and heat rises and washes through me. His tongue seeks out every heated corner of my mouth, controlling me, dominating me, and all I can do is arch into him, submitting to his power.

My hips flex over the bulge in his lap, and he groans into my mouth. His lips leave mine, dragging down the side of my neck, sucking and nipping on my flesh. My head falls back, and I struggle to breathe as his hand covers my breast, his thumb flicking over my nipple, torturing me through the fabric of my shirt and bra.

His tongue laves the skin of my throat, and I cry out as his teeth nip, delicate little prickles of pain swiftly morphing into something hot and demanding. The fabric of my shirt rubs against my sensitized skin, another kind of torture that makes me cry out, pulling at the buttons, freeing myself from the sensory overload.

His hand dips inside my bra, and I gasp as his fingers cover the hot, aching flesh of my breast, pinching and rolling my nipple. I try to move away, desperate to gain some respite, but his arm at my back is unrelenting, holding me firmly in place while I cry out in an agony of pleasure and pain, gasping for air. Heat builds within me, but it's not enough. I need more.

His hand leaves my breast, and I sob in relief, only to have my breath lock in my throat as his fingers brush over the soft skin of my thigh.

His mouth moves south over my chest while his fingers circle closer to my hot, wet center, already soaked and aching. My pussy clenches as his touch grazes the skin of my thighs, and I whimper, desperate for him to touch me where I want it most. I'm not prepared for his mouth to close over my nipple at the exact same moment his fingers slip beneath the band of my panties and thrust into my pussy.

I arch in his arms, held prisoner by the steel band of his arm at my back, his mouth on my breast, rolling my nipple between his teeth, and his fingers inside me, sliding and curling to hit *that spot* with every stroke while his thumb flirts with my clit, circling it until I'm practically climbing out of my skin.

Sobbing with desperation, I can only moan and gasp and whimper in his arms as every touch, every lick, every slick sliding motion of his hand coils my need tighter within me, hardening it to diamond sharpness until suddenly, it explodes, my orgasm tearing me apart as my screams echo in the enclosed space of the car.

I collapse against him, gasping for breath, and gradually float back into myself. Eventually, I raise my head from his shoulder, to find myself staring into those dark blue eyes. Desire slithers in my belly once more, my core tightening as he slides his fingers out of me, then licks them clean. Mesmerized by his lips and tongue on his own skin, I lean in to kiss him and taste myself on his mouth.

His hand fists in my hair, drawing my head back so that he can lay another trail of hot, open-mouthed kisses down the side of my throat and I shiver in his grip. His other arm remains locked around my waist, and all I can do is flex my hips against the bulge in his groin, gasping as it hits my clit. I'm still sensitive from our previous go-around so it doesn't take much to have me right on the edge of another orgasm, but suddenly, he lifts his head, and I freeze.

Did I do something wrong?

"We're here, sir." A voice comes through the intercom, and I belatedly realize the car has stopped. That must be what made...

Oh my God. I don't even know this guy's name. How is that even possible?

His arms loosen around me, and I fly off his lap, pulling at my clothes, fumbling with buttons. His eyes darken and he reaches for me, but at that moment, the door opens, and I scramble out of the car and run as fast as I can.

***

Keeley

I run until my lungs are screaming and I can't breathe. Then I duck into a cafe and race into their bathroom, locking the door behind me and staring at my reflection in the mirror.

Face flushed, eyes too wide and too bright, hair standing on end... Yeah, I look like I've had a screaming orgasm in the last half hour.

Or like a crazy person. I'm not sure which is worse, considering I'm supposed to be continuing the search for gainful employment.

Damn him. *Damn him!* Why did he have to, to...

Drag you into his car and give you the best orgasm of your life?

Yes! That! Okay, so the orgasm was on a whole new plane of spectacular, but how the hell am I supposed to go job-hunting looking like this?

I shake my head. I have no choice. I need a job and today is Friday. The kinds of places I want to work at, the big corporate firms, won't be open over the weekend. I need to just get over this...aberration...and move on. Preferably into a goddamn job.

I carefully ignore the thought that keeps smirking at me from the back of my mind. That guy, that sinfully gorgeous guy, may have dragged me into his car, but I didn't fight him off. I didn't even complain. Never tried to get free, or escape the car.

I crawled into his lap and came all over his hand.

If he's a bad guy for pulling me in there in the first place, what does that make me?

I take a deep breath, then let it out through my nose. A few more of those, and my reflection definitely looks a lot less insane. *Good.* I nod to myself. Time to hit the pavement.

I open the door, and I'm immediately assaulted by the rich aroma of coffee, accompanied by the scent of various pastries.

Maybe I'll take a coffee first. It'll help ground me. Or something.

"Oh, to hell with it," I mutter as I head for the counter. "I deserve coffee."

I pay for my drink and head for the door, but halfway there I pass a table occupied by a couple of girls around my age, one of them looking on the verge of tears.

"So you quit?" asks the non-teary one.

"I had to," sniffles her friend. "I couldn't take one more minute of that asshole dictating to me. And the way he looked at me. Like he knew what color underwear I was wearing."

My skin prickles. I remember being looked at like that, just a few minutes ago. Not that I'd been complaining.

"No wonder he has such a hard time keeping an

assistant over there. I thought everyone was exaggerating when they said no one in their right mind will work for him, but they weren't. If anything, they were sugarcoating it. Now what do I do?"

Her friend handed her a pastry. "Eat. And wave goodbye to Vulpus Industries. You're the best. You can get a job anywhere in this town, don't worry about it."

Vulpus Industries.

Thanks for the tip.

I slide out onto the street and do a quick search on my phone. Vulpus Industries is only a couple of blocks away. Another search, this time on some of the admin workers forums, tells me the girl's story pans out. Evidently Caden Fox, the CEO, is a total ass, a nightmare to work with. I grin when I see that.

Means less competition for the position.

I head for Vulpus Industries, using the walk to put my game face on. They need an assistant, and I need a job. No matter how bad this guy is, I won't walk away. I can't. He can't be worse than Wallis.

The receptionist looks shocked when I tell her I'm here about the executive assistant position, but hides it fast. I'm guessing she doesn't want to scare anyone off. A few minutes later, an older woman with dark grey hair picks me up in the lobby and leads me towards an elevator. She smells very faintly of gardenias, my favorite flower, and it helps me relax.

"I was surprised to find an applicant walking in so soon," she admits as she presses the call button. "I hadn't even called the agency yet."

She levels a stare at me, and for some reason, I like her. She looks like she doesn't take any shit, and I can respect that. I figure at this point, it hurts no one if I tell the truth.

"I'm in the market for a job, and I overheard a conversation indicating there was a vacancy."

She raises an eyebrow. "I can imagine. Then you're aware this is a highly demanding position?"

"I'm aware." The elevator arrives, and we step in.

Instead of pushing a button, she presses the close doors button, then turns to me. "I'll be frank. He's very difficult to work with. We need someone who can handle him, and the job, for longer than a week without running out the door in tears."

I can't help smiling. She doesn't return the expression. Probably thinks I'm not taking her seriously. I figure the truth is worth a shot.

"Look," I tell her. "I don't have the luxury of running away from a job. I'm out of money, and I'm out of time. If I'm going to cover my rent this month, I need to work. I don't care if you've got Shrek's wicked stepmother up there. I'm not going anywhere."

It's slight but I catch it; the faintest twitch at the corner of her mouth. So Steel Gardenia has a sense of humor, even about her boss. Good to know.

"I'll bear that in mind," she says. "Resumé?"

She presses another button, and the elevator starts to rise. I hand her my resumé, and she looks it over. I know it's a little thin on high level corporate experience, but she doesn't seem to mind.

The elevator stops, and we step out, my shoes

sinking into luxurious carpet. She leads me across a wide, open office area, gesturing at a door on the left.

"His office. Do not go in unless expressly invited to do so, and never open the door when it is closed."

I nod.

She walks through another door and sits behind a large desk. "You'll find this is a few steps up from what you're used to, but I think you can handle it. It takes a hell of a lot of spine to sign up for a job like this, even in your...circumstances. You're going to need all the spine you can get."

For the first time, apprehension twists in my belly, tight and cold. *Too late now,* I remind myself. Besides, I really don't have any other option. I *need* a job.

She picks something out of her desk, then heads for the door again. "Come. We'll get you settled, and you can meet your new boss."

I follow her back out into the open office area, and she gestures at a large desk which faces the boss's door. "This will be your workstation. Please fill out these forms. I'll get them sent down to HR, and I'll also see about getting you an advance on your first pay, if that would be helpful?"

I stare at her, my mouth falling open with shock. "Y-yes. Thank you!"

She brushes off my thanks with a wave of her hand. "If you leave inside the first pay period, you'll have to pay it back. Are we clear?"

I start to smile, then straighten my face. She's making sure I stick around for at least a few weeks. That's fair enough. "Very clear."

"Good. I'm Sheridan, by the way." She holds out a hand, and we shake.

"Keeley," I tell her out of habit, even though she already knows from my resume. "Keeley Gant."

"Keeley," says another voice, and I freeze, liquid ice tumbling down my spine even as heat unfurls inside me to wrap around my pussy.

No. No way.

But when I look up, my eyes clash with a dark blue gaze that has my nipples hardening on the spot.

"Mr. Fox, this is your new assistant. Keeley Gant, meet Caden Fox, the CEO of Vulpus Industries."

I can barely hear Sheridan's voice over the roaring in my ears as she introduces me to the man who made me come in his car not an hour ago.

Caden

My first thought when I see her is, *how did she find me?* One look at her pale face tells me she's as surprised as I am to find she's working in the same building as me, let alone the same office.

She doesn't look overjoyed at the prospect, but I'm ecstatic. Not that I can show it. Sheridan knows of my proclivities, but I have always maintained a professional demeanor in the office. It helps that I've never been in the slightest bit interested in any of my assistants.

Until now.

"Gant, is it?" I ask, adopting my snappish, boardroom tone.

"Yes, sir," she says, her grey eyes meeting mine with a hint of challenge.

Something in my chest relaxes. She's not a pushover. Two words, and she's already showing more strength than some of her predecessors demonstrated throughout their tenure in this office. Not that any of them ever lasted long.

But Keeley will.

I hope.

"In my office," I bark at her. "Letters."

"Certainly, sir." She turns and picks up a pad and a pen, and I take a moment to admire the way her ass fills out her skirt as she bends over her desk, even as my cock aches.

That's a view I intend to see more often, only she'll be wearing nothing but stockings and a silk thong. A drenched, silk thong, which I'll rip off—

"Sir?"

I blink. They're both staring at me, and I glare back, discomfited to have been caught openly fantasizing about my new assistant. I spin around and stalk into my office. "Today, Miss Gant!"

I can practically hear her rolling her eyes behind me, and I smile at the window. This is going to be fun.

***

An hour later, I've discovered that Keeley's mind is almost as attractive as her body. She's relaxed and calm as I fire letters at her, her pen racing over her notebook in elegant shorthand. She makes eye contact without attempting to flirt, and I find myself wishing she would, just so I could punish her for it.

I send her back to her desk with a dozen letters to type up, fully anticipating it taking up the rest of her day, and attempt manfully to focus on the day's work. It's a hopeless task. I stare at my computer screen, and all I can see is her bent over my desk, her ass offered up for my hands, my mouth, my cock...

The phone buzzes on my desk, and I pick up. "What?"

"Mr. Lupin for you, sir."

"Who said I was interested in taking calls?" I snap at her, even though I know exactly who Lupin is.

"He's on Sheridan's list of pre-approved callers, sir. She was very specific."

As well she might be, since Max Lupin has been my best friend since kindergarten.

"Put him through, then," I bark at her. She doesn't seem fazed, though, simply connects the call.

"Mr. Lupin for you, sir," she says, without a trace of temper, before hanging up.

"What do you want, Max?"

Max laughs. "Can't a man call an old friend?"

I wait, flicking idly through my inbox. He'll get to the point sooner if I make him stew.

"Fine. I heard you had a new assistant, and I just had to find out how long the previous one lasted. I'm sure she was new the last time I called, and that was three hours ago."

Max is always giving me shit about how I run through assistants. He doesn't understand my need for control, nor my wish to be met halfway.

"She was a petulant child. Keeley is far more mature, even though she's younger."

"Keeley, is it? I think that's the first time I've ever heard you refer to one of your assistants by their first name."

I grit my teeth. Trust Max to pick up on a detail like that. It's what makes him such a brilliant venture capitalist, but it's a pain in the ass in a friend, especially one you don't want sharking on your new assistant.

"Nothing to say?" he teases.

"What do you want, Max? It's the middle of the day. I'm busy."

He sighs theatrically. "You're no fun today. Okay, fine. Were you planning on working late tonight?"

I huff out a laugh. "I work as late as I need to, you know that."

"Good. An opportunity has come up, and I think it might be a good fit for you. Problem is, they're trying to rush us through the process, got a bunch of us on the hook, wanting in on the first round. I haven't got the paperwork yet, but when I do, it'll need an extra pair of eyes. I doubt they'll give us more than twenty-four hours to go over it."

Not for nothing is Max one of the richest men in the country. If he thinks it's a good fit, it probably is, and I never turn down a good fit.

The thought makes me think of how I'll fit inside Keeley, and I tear my mind away before I can get sidetracked with thoughts of her tight, wet pussy gripping my cock like a vice.

"Sounds good. I look forward to seeing it."

I end the call, and a moment later, Keeley

appears in my doorway. The sight of her curvy figure makes my cock throb, and I lean back in my chair to cover the movement of me adjusting myself beneath the desk.

"What is it?" I bark at her. She doesn't flinch. Damn, what does it take to get this woman nervous?

And then I remember. My hand around her wrist this morning, her licking her lips... She may not be a pushover, but she likes to be controlled. I hide my smile. This is going to be fun.

"I need you to sign these letters, sir," she says, sashaying across the room to place the letters on my desk.

I blink. Twelve letters, some several pages long, sit in a neat stack on my desk. I read them through, one by one. They're all perfect. I frown up at her. She's biting her lip. She's nervous. This is the first time I've seen her nervous. Well, since this morning's encounter in the car.

"Good work," I say, picking up the pen and signing each one, and she relaxes, just a tiny amount. Good, I want her off guard. "We'll be working late most evenings. Make sure you're prepared."

"How late is late?" she asks, her musical voice tugging at something deep inside me.

I glare at her to hide how much she's turning me on. "As late as I say," I snap. "Is that a problem?"

"No," she says, a little too quickly. There's a story there, and I'm going to uncover it. "But what if I have to get home? Maybe I have a dog. I can't just leave him on his own half the night as well as all day."

I raise an eyebrow. "Do you have a dog?"

She hesitates for a moment, chewing on her full lower lip, before replying. "No. My life's too...up in the air. A dog is a big commitment. I can't take that on at the moment. Do you?"

I frown. I was so focused on her teeth worrying the plump flesh of her lip that I lost the thread of what she was saying. "Do I what?"

"Have a dog," she says, displaying a hint of the temper I suspect she's doing her best to hide.

"Oh. No, no, I don't. It is indeed a big commitment. I love dogs, but I've never felt settled enough to get one. I travel a lot for work, not to mention putting in long hours even when I am in the city. Hours which my assistant is expected to put in as well."

Her eyebrows draw together slightly before she makes a clear effort to smooth her face out. My palms itch with the need to touch her, caress her soft skin. I barely catch the small movement of her hips, but I recognize it immediately. She's pressing her thighs together, which means she's already wet and aching for me. I can't wait any longer.

I set the letters aside, then eye the open door behind her, before sitting back and looking at my computer screen. I frown, as though seeing something which displeases me. "Close the door, then come and look at this, would you?"

She hesitates for just a second before turning to shut the door. She rounds the desk and leans close to get a look at the screen. "What are we looking at?"

I wrap my arm around her waist and nudge her sideways and forwards, so that she sprawls across my desk. She cries out in surprise, then gasps as I stand behind her, my cock nestled against her ass, hard and demanding to be released.

Keeley

I'm bent over his desk, my hands scrabbling for purchase against the oak surface, trying to figure out what just happened, when he stands up behind me, and I feel him, or rather his erection. He's hard against the crack of my ass, and all the air leaves my lungs.

My pussy has been throbbing since I found out I'm now working with the same guy who made me come so hard this morning. I can't show it, been trying really hard not to. The last thing I want is for him to think I somehow engineered all this. I can't cope with another man ruining my life, yet again, even if he wouldn't actually be wrong to fire me as soon as he recognized me.

He didn't seem happy about it, but it's not my job to make him happy. It's my job to do as I'm told and get the work done. I'm sure as hell not going to give him any excuse to fire me.

Right now, though, getting fired is the last thing on my mind. My panties have been damp all day, but now they're soaked, my arousal curling through me, hot and wet and desperate. I've never felt like this before, like I'm so desperate to feel a cock inside me, my pussy is spasming with need.

"Sir?" I say, my voice shaky and breathless.

"That's right," he growls. "I'm Sir. Don't forget it."

The animalistic sound of his voice, dark and hard as a gravel pit, rasps over my clit like a physical touch, making me arch and gasp. "No, sir."

"Good girl."

For a moment, I wonder if he's about to let me up, but then his hands skim up the sides of my legs, and I quiver. He's not letting me up any time soon, and I'm *glad*.

"I'm impressed, Keeley," he says. "So far, you're a very good assistant. A very good girl."

"Th-thank you, sir." His hands dip under the hem of my skirt and continue to rise, sliding the fabric up over my hips. Cool air washes over my wet panties, and I shiver with a blend of embarrassment and desire.

"You weren't a good girl this morning, though, were you?" His fingers brush across my lower back, leaving my skirt around my waist, and I struggle to focus on what he's saying as goosebumps spring up in the wake of his touch.

"I-I wasn't?"

His open palm cracks down on my ass cheek, and I shriek as pain blossoms across my flesh.

"No, you weren't. I gave you pleasure, and you ran from me." His hand smacks my other ass cheek, and I cry out again, even as my face flames.

He never got his, and he's mad at me. Of course he is. That's like, the unspoken agreement, right? A guy gets you off, and he gets off in return? Whoops. He's not to know I'm a virgin. Although I guess that won't be lasting much longer. He's entitled to think he's got a right to fuck me. I brace myself. This is going to hurt.

"I'm really sorry, sir," I tell him, trying to swallow back my tears. "Are you going to take yours now?"

He freezes behind me, and I tense up, waiting for the invasion I know is coming.

But it doesn't come. Instead, I'm suddenly pulled off the desk, spun around, and pressed back against it as he looms over me.

"What kind of asshole do you think I am?"

My mouth goes dry as I stare up at him. I don't think he's an asshole at all, but right now, with him so close I can see flecks of brown in his eyes, I'm too turned on to say so. This is insane. I should be terrified, and yet my skin prickles, and my belly is tight, my pussy clenching with *need*. I want this man, *need* him, like I've never needed anyone.

"I don't think you're an asshole," I breathe. "But that's why you're mad at me, right? Cos you didn't get yours…" I trail off as fury snaps in his eyes.

"What kind of ignorant oafs have you been associating with?" he barks. "I'm upset because I wasn't finished making you come. I wanted you limp, spent, boneless from all the orgasms I'd given you. I wanted you so pleasured that you couldn't remember your own name, but you'd remember mine because you'd screamed it so many times, the walls rang with it. That's why I'm upset."

"Oh."

I can't think. I can barely breathe. The images conjured up by his words have me ready to climb up and impale myself on his cock right now.

But now I don't know what to say. I'm such an idiot. He's probably going to want to get rid of me now, and just when I've found the perfect job, that apparently comes with built-in orgasms, I'm going to lose it again.

Frustration brings tears to my eyes, and I bite my lip to hold back a sob.

"Hey." He lifts a hand to my face, his thumb brushing away tears from beneath my eye in an unexpectedly gentle caress. "I'm sorry. I thought you were onboard with this. We can stop. It's not a prob—"

I stare at him, then grab his shirt with both hands, and pull him down so that I can meld my mouth to his. His lips are firm and hot beneath mine, and my belly flips, desire sliding within me. Then he takes control, his tongue slicking into my mouth to dominate every part of it, bending me back over the desk in the process. I cling to him, one of my hands sliding up his chiseled chest to tunnel into his hair. I revel in hard muscle and thick, silky strands, but then his hands cover mine, and he's pulling me away from him.

"I'm confused. We're not doing this?"

"We are doing this," he murmurs in my ear as he turns me around and bends me over the desk in the exact same position as before. "We're just going to do it my way."

The air locks up in my lungs, and I can't even breathe, let alone speak. Should I tell him I'm a virgin? Jason acted like it was the most pathetic thing imaginable, and I really don't want to make him stop again.

He leans over me and slides a thin circle up out of the top of his desk. It's lined with velvet and it's only when he closes it around my wrist that I can tell what it is. A cuff. He's cuffing me to his desk.

I whimper, but then his breath tickles my ear. He lifts my hair away from my neck, then kisses his way down to my shoulder. Hot, wet kisses that leave me squirming with desire, my body straining to get closer to him.

"All in good time, little one," he says, stroking one hand down my back in a gesture that sets my nerves on fire, making me arch up into his touch. His fingers slide down over my ass and he draws my panties down my legs. "So wet. So sensitive to my touch. One would almost think you were a virgin."

"Well, yeah," I gasp, then freeze. Shit. *Shit.*

He's still for a moment, then he leans over me. "Is there anything else you need to tell me?"

Burning with embarrassment for the second time, I squeeze my eyes shut and shake my head.

"Say it out loud, Keeley. And look at me when you speak to me."

I swallow and open my eyes. He's right there, so close, I could fall into his eyes and never come up. "Nothing else," I whisper.

"Good."

His hands glide down over my ass, parting my cheeks so that he can follow my crack right down to my asshole. I yelp as his finger dips inside, probing, testing. It feels so naughty, so *forbidden*, and yet so gloriously full of potential.

"You like that, Keeley?" he asks.

I gasp out a 'yes'.

"Noted."

His finger continues on lower, sliding through the wet curls covering my pussy, making me moan as his touch brushes over the needy, aching core of me. Then he finds my clit and *presses,* and I wail as pleasure spikes through me, an orgasm taking me by surprise and tearing me apart with just that one touch.

I've barely got my breath back when his finger slides inside my pussy, making me moan. With his spare hand, he turns my face so that he can kiss me, his tongue thrusting into my mouth in counterpoint to his finger inside me. I can't get my breath. I'm trapped between his body and the desk, and I don't care. My entire world has narrowed to his mouth and his hands and what they're doing to me.

A second finger pushes inside me, making me shriek into his mouth, and he leans in close, his hips pressing his cock against my bare ass. The fabric of his pants rubs against skin still sensitive from the spanking he gave me, his movement pressing me against the desk as his fingers inside me hit even more pleasurable places. I cry out with every stroke until suddenly, I'm screaming as another orgasm rips through me, lighting the world on fire and drowning me in a rainbow of color.

I lie there, gasping, trembling, and he reaches over me and undoes the cuffs. He slides my limp body towards him, then turns me over, so that I'm lying on the desk with my legs on either side of his chair. He reattaches the cuffs, pinning my hands to the desk above my head, then pulls me closer to him, so that my hips are right on the edge of the oak slab, and he looks at me up the length of my body.

"I've been wondering what you taste like all

day." And with that, he buries his face in my pussy, and I scream again. His tongue slides in and out of my channel before licking up over my clit, torturing it with light flicks and flat strokes, his hands holding me in place as I buck and writhe in his arms. Another orgasm whips through me, swiftly followed by another, and another, until I lose count of the number of times I've come. At some point, he insists I use his first name, and I scream it so many times that by the time I slide into darkness, I know I'll never forget it.

***

Keeley

I float home on a cloud of post-orgasmic bliss, alternating between wondering how long it's going to be before all this crashes down around my ears, because I'm not stupid enough to think a workplace fling with a billionaire is going to end well, and not caring one way or the other. Because, well, I mentioned that post-orgasmic bliss, right?

I've never done anything like this before. Hell, I always looked down on women who sleep their way to the top. Except, now it occurs to me they might not have needed to. Maybe they just got dragged into a lust-filled encounter and figured screaming orgasms were the perfect antidote to a stressful work day.

From where I'm standing, they weren't wrong.

Not that working for Caden is desperately stressful. It's more that it's always changing. He doesn't even take his coffee a certain way; it's a different order every time. Still, I like variety, and the novelty of orgasming on my boss's desk totally works for me.

Even the sight of my crappy building isn't enough to drain the smile from my face. Sheridan was as good as her word. Half my first pay is already in my account, and it's more than enough to cover my rent. It's also nearly as much as the highest monthly salary I've ever had before now. When I queried it with Sheridan, she just gave me a pitying smile and pointed out I was working in the CEO's office. They pay those people well.

Grinning like a loon, I waltz into the lobby, practically dancing on air as I check my mailbox. Another couple of job rejections, but it doesn't matter. I have a job. A great job. One with unexpected perks. Today is great.

I turn around and walk smack into Wallis. Damn, I'm slipping. I was so caught up in red-hot memories of today's desktop shenanigans that I hadn't been paying attention to my surroundings. That's unforgivably stupid. You can't let your guard down around here, not with assholes like Wallis around.

He steps into me, and I back up, only to come up hard against the mailboxes. The look in his eyes is cold and calculating, and in no way reflects the smile on his lips.

"How you doing today, Keeley? Need help with your rent?"

His breath smells so bad, I can't keep from scrunching up my nose against the terrible odor. His eyes narrow, and my heart sinks. Oh no. This isn't looking so good.

"Think you're so much better than all of us, don't you? Like a suit makes you worth more than me." He hooks his finger into the top of my shirt, wiggling it down to brush against my breasts. I recoil from his touch, or try to, but there's nowhere to go. He leers at me, revealing yellowed, broken teeth, and leans in, wet lips covering mine. My cry of disgust is a mistake, allowing him to force his tongue into my mouth.

Something snaps inside me, and I bite down, hard.

Now it's his turn to recoil, hand over his mouth, before his other hand swings out, cracking across my face with enough force to knock me into the wall.

"You furgin bish!" he slurs, unable to enunciate clearly with his swollen tongue, his eyes watering with pain. He lurches towards me, and I dodge around him, heading up the stairs as fast as I can.

When I'm safely on the next flight, I yell down the stairs at him. "You'll have your rent on time, asshole!"

And then I run up the stairs to my apartment and slam the door, sliding home every single bolt before pushing the heaviest piece of furniture Jason left me, a small dresser, in front of the door. I slide down to sit on the floor, my back to the dresser, and do my best to swallow my tears. I wouldn't put it past Wallis to come and listen at the damn door, and I can't let him know he got to me.

Nor can I lose this job. I need to get out of here, but first I'll need at least three months rent in the bank, if not six, because Wallis sure as hell isn't going to give me a reference. I pull out my phone and start searching for new apartments, keeping my new pay grade in my head as I look at rental prices.

Three months. Maybe four, to be safe. That's how long I need to keep this job at Vulpus before I can afford a new place. My stomach turns over. I don't know if I can hold Wallis off for that long.

My jaw aches. I'm gritting my teeth. Damn it. I'll buy a goddamn taser if I have to. Wallis isn't getting any more of me than he already has, and I will be out of here in record time. I can keep living on ramen if I have to. It won't kill me in the next six months, which is how long it'll take me to make rent on a new place and get enough money in the bank to be able to afford proper food again.

I can do it. I've been in worse situations. And now I've got an awesome job, with an awesome boss. Just thinking about him makes my breasts tingle and my stomach melt, and I get up and head for the pantry to pick out tonight's flavor of ramen feast. I can do this.

And if I have to leave the noodles cooking while I lie on my bed and rub one out to take the edge off my arousal, well, it's not the worst consequence of having an unimaginably sexy boss.

***

Caden

One of the privileges of owning one's own company is an open line to HR on the personal details of one's employees. I usually leave all that to Sheridan, but I'm more than happy to abuse this particular privilege when it comes to Keeley. Which is why I'm sitting in the back of my car, grimacing at the outside of her building at half past seven the following morning.

Being a billionaire certainly comes with a number of benefits, one being not having to live in a shithole like this. The building looks as though one strong wind will send it crashing to the ground, killing everyone inside, and my gut clenches at the thought of Keeley being among them. I frown at the window. Maybe I can find a way to give her a bonus that will allow her to leave now, rather than having to wait until she can afford first and last month's rent on a new place.

Of course, in an ideal world, she'd move into my place, but since we work together, in the unlikely event that I ever tire of her, it could make for a messy situation. Better to help her move on to a better place of her own. Besides, she will no doubt eventually tire of me. Sex, as I have discovered, only takes one so far in a relationship, and I've always been terrible at the other aspects. My life is dedicated to my business, although since Keeley walked through the door, I seem to be finding more and more reasons to focus on her instead of the day to day running of my company.

I should be focusing on getting my head back in the game, focusing on this upcoming 'opportunity' Max is sending my way. Keeley will be helpful in terms of looking over the paperwork… and there it is again. My brain inserting her into my work day.

"She's your assistant, you idiot. Of course she's part of your work day."

"Sir?"

Parker's voice over the intercom is mildly troubled, and I bite my tongue to keep from snapping at him. Now is not the time for him to think his boss is losing it. Talking to myself, experiencing mood swings. Parker has worked for enough top executives to know what drug usage looks like. On one hand, he's my employee and his opinion of me should therefore be of no concern. But he's been with me for a long time now, and I respect him. Not to mention, if I lose it in front of him, it's only a matter of time before my lack of focus shows in the boardroom, and that is unacceptable.

"Nothing," I tell him, and look back out the window in time to see Keeley emerge from the lobby of her building. I can't keep my smile off my face, but it fades as a man follows her and grabs her arm, pushing her against the doorframe. He appears to have something intimate in mind. I can see it on his face, and I stiffen. Is she taken? Did she willingly whore herself out to get a good job? Except that makes no sense. She didn't even know who I was the first time we met, and even if she had, how was she to know our encounter was at least partially due to my previous assistant quitting on me after I got frustrated with her lack of business knowledge, thereby paving the way for Keeley to step in.

I shake my head. Years of being pursued by women has soured me against them to a certain extent, and when I take a breath and look at Keeley's face, her expression has me opening the door to the car and stepping onto the sidewalk.

The movement attracts their attention, and

Keeley takes advantage of her assailant's distraction to duck away from him and hurry towards me. Whoever he is, he sees the look on my face and stays exactly where he is. Smart man, to a degree. I know when Parker emerges from the car, because whoever the asshole in the doorway is, he goes pale and melts back into the shadows of the building's interior.

Keeley smiles at me, and I frown. It's a fake smile, and I hate them. I see far too many in my line of work, all pretense and bluff. It irritates me when people aren't honest about their feelings. I thought she and I were beyond that point. My annoyance morphs into genuine concern, however, when I see the dark shadows under her eyes which she hasn't quite been able to hide with makeup.

"Is everything okay?" I ask, well aware my voice is rougher than it should be, a combination of worry and lust darkening my tones. The woman looks entirely too good in a suit, but the distraction is minor. I find myself unusually concerned over her wellbeing, a new situation for me. The women I usually associate with are more than able to take care of themselves, but Keeley is different. For one thing, those other women can afford to live in buildings which aren't one step away from demolition.

"Fine," she says, that fake smile barely cracking. I see it, though, the stress beneath the facade. Like this building, she appears to be hanging on by a thread. "What are you doing here? And how many cars do you have? Do you ride in a different one every day?"

I consider pushing the matter, forcing her to tell

me what the problem is, and why that man thought he had the right to put his hands on her, but I dismiss the idea. She doesn't know me well enough yet to trust me, and if that's the kind of man she's associating with, I can see why. My pride is a little offended to be lumped in with such a low class specimen, but I can take the hit. If she wants to focus on business, we can do that, too. Eventually, she'll trust me, and then she'll allow me to take care of her. In more ways than one.

The thought has my cock hardening in my pants, and I turn away to hide my need to adjust it.

"I own a number of cars, and I consider it a waste not to use them all. I also consider variety the spice of life."

Her chest rises as she drags in a breath. The flush of arousal on her cheeks causes a stream of hot thoughts to tumble through my brain, and my cock grows impossibly harder. This woman is going to kill me.

"A friend called yesterday with an investment opportunity. Today, we're going to his place to look over the paperwork. It's a tight deadline, so we need as many eyes as possible. I thought it would make more sense for me to pick you up so we could go straight there."

"Oh. Okay."

I watch her settle into the soft leather seat, gradually relaxing after whatever went down just now.

"Who was that?" I ask, failing utterly to keep my voice casual. I want to rip the fucker's head from his shoulders for scaring her. For scaring me. For the first time, I admit, if only to myself, that I care more for Keeley than most of my...companions. There's something innocent about her, more than the virginity she offered me so carelessly. My jaw tightens as I imagine the guy in her building taking it instead. He clearly wants to.

He hasn't a hope.

Not if I have anything to say in the matter.

"Who was what?" she asks, flipping through the itinerary I left on her seat, and I frown at her.

"Don't play games with me," I snap. "The man who frightened you outside your building just now. The one manhandling you, or are there so many these days you're losing track?"

Her head whips up and she stares at me, mouth open. For just a moment, she looks scared, like a rabbit about to run, and then I see the glint of steel as her temper asserts itself. I hide my smile. I much prefer her angry to scared.

"He's my landlord, and my relationship with him is none of your business. Now, is there anything I need to know about Max Lupin before we get to his place?"

I open my mouth to argue, but my words die in my throat. "How do you know we're going to see Max?"

She gives me a look that makes me want to put her over my knee. "The only friend who called you yesterday was Max Lupin. Therefore…"

She raises an eyebrow at me, then goes back to the itinerary. I stare at her, my cock demanding to be buried inside her, my mouth watering with the need to taste her again, and I can't resist any longer. I reach out and drag her onto my lap, covering her mouth with mine to absorb her yelp of surprise. She struggles briefly against me, but I turn her so that her back is to my chest, running my hand up between her thighs to brush over the damp cotton covering her pussy.

She gasps, her head falling back on my shoulder, and I press my advantage, flicking open buttons on her blouse until I can slide my other hand inside, drawing circles over the tops of her breasts, the twin mounds heaving as she fights for air. I pull her bra down, freeing her nipple for my thumb to tease, and she moans against my ear.

Her nipples are already hard, much like my cock, currently lengthening against the soft weight of her ass. I flex my hips against her while pressing harder into the dampness between her legs, and I'm rewarded with a moan.

She raises a hand, and I grab her wrist, directing her fingers to wrap around the cushion beneath us. "And your other hand," I mutter in her ear. Satisfaction roars within me when she does as she's told. She's perfect.

I torture her nipple, rolling it between my thumb and forefinger, rewarded with whimpers and moans, while my other hand continues to brush back and forth over her increasingly wet panties.

"Please?" she begs, her voice thready with need.

"Don't speak," I tell her, secure in the knowledge she won't be able to stay silent for long. I squeeze her nipple, then flick it with my thumb, reveling in the sound of her breathing, her soft flesh warm against me, the heady power of her surrender to my touch.

The heat between her legs is a siren call I can no longer resist, and I tease the edge of her panties before slipping a finger beneath the cotton to drag through the nectar gathering beneath. She groans, her spine arching. I avoid her clit, content to graze my finger over her softest skin in the lightest of touches, barely brushing over her pussy lips, back and forth, back and forth.

She writhes in my arms, trying to press closer, desperate for more contact, and I pinch her nipple, making her shriek with pain and pleasure.

"Please, oh please," she says, unable to hold back any more, and I smile, pleasure roaring within me.

I lift her and rearrange her over my lap, pushing her skirt up around her waist, dragging my fingers through the soft curls covering her pussy as I go.

She bucks against me, and I hold her in place with one hand at the back of her neck, while my other hand strokes circles over her ass cheeks.

"Did you hear me tell you not to speak?" I ask, caressing her soft, supple skin.

"Yes," she moans.

"Why did you disobey me?"

"I-I-I couldn't, please, I just, I just—"

Her cry echoes around the inside of the car as I bring my palm down on her ass. I rub her skin, admiring the pink tone, then smack her again. Her body jerks beneath me, teasing my cock, which is already hard as a rock. I spank her again and again, reveling in her shrieks and the rosy glow taking over her ass. When I'm satisfied, I run my fingers down her ass crack, pushing her panties aside and sliding two fingers into her soaking pussy in one fluid movement.

She cries out as I thrust into her, over and over, until her pussy clenches around my hand like a vice, rippling up and down my fingers as her orgasm rocks through her, leaving her limp and spent across my thighs.

***

Keeley

It's been a long day, going over paperwork which I barely understand. Or rather, I barely understood it when we got started. Nine hours later, I'm starting to get a handle on it. Max doesn't seem to mind my questions and is always happy to explain stuff. He is also a spectacularly good-looking guy, and the way my boss growls at him every time our hands meet on pieces of paper, Caden's aware of it too.

It doesn't matter. Max just laughs easily every time it happens, and I'm not even slightly interested in him. Not when I have increasing numbers of scorching hot memories involving my boss's hands and mouth on my body, making me scream over and over. I've lost track of the number of orgasms he's given me. When we took a break for lunch, he dragged me out to the gardens stretching over acres of land behind Max's mansion, sat me down on a bench, and ate me out until I screamed for mercy.

He didn't give me any, of course. Mercy, that is. My voice was hoarse by the time we went back in, Max's knowing look making me flush with embarrassment. By now, nearly nine o'clock at night, I can barely speak at all. Not that I mind. I'm tired, but relaxed. Orgasms are a fantastic way to de-stress.

Now we're back in Caden's car, heading back into the city, and I'm fighting sleep.

"Time for dinner, I think," says Caden next to me, as I try not to pass out.

"Yes, please," I rasp, then grimace. My frown deepens as I see him trying not to smile. "It's your fault!"

"I know," he says, reaching out to brush a strand of hair off my face. "I'm not complaining. I love seeing you lose control, especially when it's because of me."

I narrow my eyes at him but open them again immediately. Even that small movement has my eyes wanting to close properly and give in to sleep, and I can't do that in the back of my boss's car.

"How come you're single?" he asks, and I sigh. Of all the questions he could have asked when I was exhausted and had no defenses left, he had to go with that one. "You're beautiful, intelligent, possessed of a stunningly perfect body, a spine of steel, and an excellent sense of humor. Are the men in this city blind?"

"I wasn't a week ago," I say. I'm vaguely aware he just paid me a ton of compliments, but I'm too tired to get excited about it. I know I'm just a fling to him. I have to be. What billionaire CEO is going to genuinely be interested in a woman so poor, she has to launder her one and only work blouse every night so that it's clean the next day? I daren't use the washers and dryers in the basement of the building in case Wallis catches me there.

"What happened a week ago?" says Caden, dragging my mind back to the present moment.

"He left," I say, simply, hoping to leave it at that.

Of course, that's not possible with Caden. "There's more to it than that."

It's not even a question. He *knows*.

"How do you do that?" I ask, surprised into a state approaching wakefulness. "How do you know?"

The corner of his mouth twitches, almost the beginning of a smile.

"You tensed up, and you held your breath. Never play poker, Keeley."

I roll my eyes, but he's right. I've always been a terrible liar. "Fine. He left me and took most of our furniture and all my money with him."

There's an icy silence, and when I look at Caden, I recoil from the look of utter rage on his face.

"And where is this sterling example of humanity now?" he growls.

"I don't know," I say, edging away from him across the seat. He glares at me and drags me into his lap.

"I'm not angry at you, Keeley. I'm angry at him. What possessed him to do something so heinous, least of all to someone as lovely as you?" He strokes my hair and tucks my head under his chin. Gradually, I relax against him, listening to his heart thud beneath my ear.

"I tend to attract that sort of guy, to be honest. The boyfriend before him wasn't actually even interested in me at all. He just wanted somewhere to live where he wouldn't have to pay rent while he pretended to write a book. We'd been going out since high school, and I always thought I'd lose my virginity to him, but he slept next to me in the same bed for eight months before he met someone else. Never laid a hand on me." And hadn't that been a blow to my ego?

"Someone else?"

"Another guy," I tell him, dragging my flagging brain back to the conversation at hand. "Not like I could compete when I had the wrong equipment to start with, right? He said he'd known for a while that he was gay. He just needed a cover girlfriend while he screwed up the courage to come out."

"And you were okay with that?" His tone holds no censure, no judgement, which I'm grateful for, even if I still feel stupid that I never figured it out for myself.

"No. Well, I might have been, but he only told me the day he moved out. I didn't really get a chance to process it one way or the other. I never heard from him again."

His arms wrap around me, warm and strong, and I feel cherished, protected, *safe*. For the first time in as long as I can remember, it feels like I can rely on someone else, just for a minute.

"And you never slept with the next one." He sounds curious about that, and I squirm in his arms, but he's not about to let me go. Maybe that's part of why I feel safe with him. He wants to know me, wants to touch me. Wants to have those difficult conversations.

I huff out a sigh. "No. He didn't want to have sex with a virgin."

Caden tenses up, then tilts my head back so that

I'm forced to meet his incredulous gaze. "You're kidding me?"

I smile in spite of my embarrassment. "Nope. He wanted to take things slow."

Caden raises an eyebrow, then tucks my head back under his chin. "More likely, I'm afraid, he didn't want the complication of you getting pregnant before he was ready to rip you off."

I wince. It's a harsh thing to say, but I'm starting to think he's right. God, I have such shitty taste in men.

He slides me off his lap onto the seat beside him, just in time for my door to open. I didn't even notice the car stopping. What is it about this man that makes the entire world disappear when we're together?

He guides me into a beautiful restaurant with a hand at the small of my back. His touch burns through my blouse. It's only a small area of contact, but it feels like he's marking me as his. As we move through the dining area, everyone is in formal wear, and I'm grateful for him staying so close, keeping his hand on me, making it clear I'm with him. Otherwise, I'd feel horribly underdressed, but as it is, I don't care. A number of women look like they've eaten a lemon when they see me at his side, and their jealousy gives me confidence I wouldn't otherwise have.

He pulls out my chair, pushing the waiter aside when the poor man tries to do it, then sits down opposite me. We're handed menus, and I open it up, but find my exhausted brain can't choose.

He gives me a few minutes, but when the waiter arrives to take our order, I can only send him a helpless look. He smiles gently and hands over both our menus. "We'll both have the chicken alfredo fettucine."

"Very good, sir." The waiter hurries away, and Caden reaches out and takes my hand. I try to pull it away, well aware of the amount of attention we're getting. Of course, he refuses to let go, and eventually I give up. It's not like I actually want him to let go. I'm just very conscious that eventually this will end when he gets a better offer. It'll go easier on both of us if the entire city hasn't already labeled us an item.

"You did very well today," he tells me. "It takes a sharp intellect to grasp high finance so quickly."

I smile at him. "Thanks. My dad was a serial entrepreneur. He used to say I should know my way around a financial statement."

Thoughts of my dad bring a slight pang of sadness, and I look away.

"What happened?"

I don't even have to ask how he knows something happened. I've never known a man pay such close attention to my moods. It's highly disconcerting.

"Car accident, when I was nineteen. My mom passed away when I was three, so it was always just me and my dad. And then it was just me."

He squeezes my hand. "I'm sorry."

"Thanks. It was five years ago now, but I still miss him." I'm keen to turn the conversation onto something more cheerful, so I force a smile. "What are your plans for this weekend?"

His face darkens. "Don't do that."

I stare at him. "Do what?"

"Fake good cheer. I can tell the difference, you know. You don't have to be cheerful around me. I'd rather you were yourself."

I'm still staring at him. It's pretty much the exact opposite that every past boyfriend I've ever had has told me, and I say so.

He raises an eyebrow, then releases my hand as the waiter arrives with our food. "I think we've already established," he says, as he shakes out his napkin, "that you have terrible taste in men. Although it appears to be improving."

The wicked grin that accompanies his last words causes a rush of heat to my core, and I press my thighs together to ease the sudden ache between them while trying to twirl some really lovely fettucine around my fork without splattering sauce all over my one and only work blouse.

I'm stuffed by the time we finish our main course, but the food has perked me up a bit, and I find it easier to hold a conversation. Well, up to the point where he takes my hand and starts casually stroking his thumb across my knuckles. The motion makes my nipples hard, and I inhale sharply, shifting in my seat as my pussy clenches and my breasts tingle.

The look on his face says he knows exactly the effect he's having on me. I have no idea how I'm going to sleep after this, but I don't want it to end, so when he suggests dessert, I'm happy to say yes.

Of course, this means I have to select some highly fattening thing to eat in front of the guy who keeps putting his hands on me. I bite my lip, wondering if I can stomach a sorbet.

"How about the tiramisu?" he says, and I jump,

looking up to find the waiter standing next to our table. They're both looking at me.

Put on the spot, my brain screeches to a halt, mainly because tiramisu is my all-time favorite dessert, but not something I've eaten in front of a guy since the tenth grade, when my date at the time asked if I really wanted to eat that many calories. "Uh, okay."

I can't focus on anything except the touch of his hand on mine, and when the tiramisu arrives, I'm disappointed to see two forks. To my surprise, Caden bursts out laughing, and I stare at him, utterly confused while perfectly delighted by the rich sound of his amusement.

"What's so funny?" I ask him once he's calmed down.

"You," he chuckles. "Or rather your face, when you thought I was going to make you share your dessert. Here." He forks up some of the gorgeous treat, and holds it out to me. I try to take the fork, and he shakes his head. "Uh-uh. Hands in your lap. I've been looking forward to this all day."

"You have?"

He nods, his eyes darkening to a navy so deep they're almost black. "I want to see your lips move, and your tongue. I want to see your pleasure at the flavors, the textures. I want the satisfaction of knowing I'm giving you that, that I control your pleasure, even in this."

I swallow, my mouth suddenly dry, and fist my hands in my lap while leaning forward, mouth open. He slides the fork over my lips, and I can't help moaning as the rich flavors explode across my tongue.

He does it again, his eyes focused purely on my mouth, and again, until there's nothing left on the plate and I'm sure I'm leaving a wet spot on my seat from the havoc his heated gaze is wreaking on my pussy. I'm so turned on, I can barely sit still. I'm going to have to take the coldest shower in the history of cold showers when I get back to my apartment.

***

Caden

Seeing Keeley squirm with arousal is making me so hard, I can barely walk, but I don't let her see that. She wants my hands on her, I know, but I also know she doesn't trust me yet, not completely. She trusts me with her pleasure, and that in itself is a gift worth treasuring, but I want more. I cut the thought off before it can progress further, before I can ask myself what, exactly, it is that I want from her, and focus on settling her in the back of the car. We'll drop her home first, and then Parker will take me back to my building, where I'll probably paint the walls of my shower three times before I even have a hope of sleeping.

Her eyes are drooping but lit from within. She's wired and tired. It's not a good combination. Not for what I want. She's a virgin, and even though I know I can bring her pleasure, even in her current state, I don't want her like this. She's exhausted and needs to sleep. It would be remiss of me to take up any more of her time this evening.

She fidgets in the seat next to me, alternating

between staring at me and looking everywhere else. I pretend to reading through more of Max's documentation. If our proposal is accepted, there'll be a lot more ground to cover, and I need to make sure I have all the information at my fingertips. That said, it's impossible to concentrate with such a beautiful woman next to me. Especially one so desperate to be touched, pleasured…

Her voice is raspy with fatigue, but it's still one of the sweetest melodies I've ever heard. My cock pulses, and I'm not sure I can even look at her right now without coming in my pants. She's not the only one who needs sleep. My self-control is hanging by a thread.

"Because you're exhausted," I tell her, without lifting my head from the papers in my lap. It's the truth. It's just not all the truth.

Her 'oh' is the softest of sounds, yet it pounds the air out of my chest. I grit my teeth. How have we not arrived at her building yet? I don't recall travel through the city taking this long before.

"I'm feeling much more awake now."

I put the papers down and stare at the ceiling of the car, breathing deep, praying for strength. "Keeley, if I touch you now, I won't stop until I'm balls deep inside your hot, wet pussy, making you scream my name."

The words come out more harshly than I'd intended, but the woman is trying my patience, and she's not even doing anything. I've met any number of women who did everything they could to seduce me, and sure, I've accepted a number of invitations in my time. But there's something about Keeley's innocence that has me by the balls and won't let go. I'm beginning to think this erection will never fade.

She hasn't responded, and I finally risk looking at her. It's a mistake. She's staring at me, her face flushed with that rosy glow I've come to know so well. Arousal looks good on her, and I can't keep from reaching for her.

"Screw it," I snarl as I drag her across the seat towards me.

The car stops, and I growl. Her lips are a fraction of an inch away from mine, but I can't close the gap. If I do, I won't stop until my cock is finally drained, and in its current state, that could take weeks.

I set her away from me, as gently as I can, doing my best to ignore the look of hurt on her face. "See you tomorrow, Keeley."

The door opens behind her, and something aches in my chest as light spills into the car, revealing the shine of tears in her eyes.

I deliberately turn my attention back to my paperwork and tell myself I'm grateful when the door closes again, cutting her off from my view.

Or rather, cutting me off from hers. The deeply tinted windows allow me to watch her head into her building, shoulders slumped, without her knowing.

She'll feel better in the morning. She'll be grateful when we finally do come together that I made her wait, that I took care of her pleasure in every way I could.

I repeat this mantra to myself, eyes closed, until the car's engine starts. Then I look out the window one last time, and frown as a familiar figure lopes inside the building, the light from the lobby reflecting off his greasy hair.

I hit the intercom button without thinking. "Wait."

"Yes, sir."

I don't know if Parker saw what I saw. He's sitting on the wrong side of the vehicle. It doesn't matter, though. I say wait, he waits. That's the joy of paying people what they're worth. They do as I ask, no questions asked.

I open the door and head into the building. The elevator door has an 'Out of Order' sign on it, dusty with age. I shake my head. She really needs to get out of this place.

I take the stairs two at a time. Keeley's apartment is on the third floor, and apprehension curls in my gut. It's ridiculous. I know it's ridiculous, but I can't stop myself from racing up the stairs, my palms starting to sweat.

I hear voices before I even reach the landing, and my hands curl into fists.

"Time's up, beautiful."

"Get off me. I've got your money."

"I want more than money."

I surge onto the landing as the sleazeball's hand covers her breast, and my right hook leads the way. The guy goes flying, skidding across the dirty floor until his head runs into the wall. He pushes himself upright, his face a mask of shock. I find it hard to believe no one's ever hit him before, but his expression certainly implies it.

"What the fuck, man?"

"Yes," I snarl. "Man. As opposed to an entitled child who thinks he can take whatever he wants without permission."

His brows furrow as he tries and fails to follow what I'm saying. I shake my head. "Touch her again, and I'll rip your hands off. Is that clear enough for you?"

Blood drains from his face, making him look even more pasty, but he raises his chin. "We were just talking about rent. I'm the landlord. She owes me."

"And I told you I've got your money," snaps Keeley. She glares at him, but I can see her energy draining away. She's too tired to deal with this. What's more, she shouldn't have to. And she doesn't, not with me here.

"You owe me more than money," leers the idiot who doesn't realize he has an audience, and a powerful one at that.

"Charging your tenants in the form of sex is illegal," I grit out between my teeth, "I'm sure the police would be very happy to hear about that, as would the public health department, considering this entire building is one big code violation with a staircase running through it."

His eyes narrow on me. "Do you know who I am? Fuck off, man, you don't know who you're dealing with."

My temper roars. The frustration I've been carrying around for days, not wanting to push Keeley further than she's ready to go, has had me on edge for far longer than I'd like. I stalk towards him, vaguely aware of Keeley babbling something behind me. Whatever it is, it doesn't matter.

"I know exactly who you are. Wallis Jackson, thirty-eight years old. Born and raised in Pensacola, but you left there with two warrants outstanding against you for conspiracy to defraud. You popped up here a couple of years later, having evidently won a huge personal injury lawsuit, a lawsuit which my lawyers assure me should never have been brought as all the evidence my investigators can amass suggests you were never injured at all. You bought this building with your payout and have been running it like your own personal brothel ever since. Don't worry, Mr. Jackson. I am completely aware of who you are. Now, a far more relevant question would appear to be, do you know who I am?"

He stares at me, swallowing convulsively, saying nothing. Eventually I raise an eyebrow, and he stammers, "N-no?"

"No, indeed. Suffice to say, Mr. Jackson, I am far more man than you will ever be, and if you ever touch this woman again, I will personally see to it that you spend the rest of your short, miserable life behind bars, serving as someone else's chew toy. Do I make myself clear?"

An acrid scent fills the air, and a dark stain spreads across the front of his cheap khakis. I take grim satisfaction in it. It's been a long time since I lost my temper, but I regret nothing. No one hurts what's mine.

"Keeley," I say, without taking my eyes off Jackson. "Pack whatever you need. We're leaving."

"We are?"

"Keeley," I growl, the single word the only warning she needs. Her footsteps clatter away up the next flight of stairs, and she returns a few minutes later, minutes I spend looming over

Jackson, silently daring him to move.

"I'm ready," she says.

"Don't forget me," I murmur to Jackson. "Because I won't forget you."

I turn and take her small duffel bag, escorting her down the stairs with a hand at the small of her back, my jaw aching where I've gritted my teeth too long.

As we leave the lobby, she whispers to me, "You made him piss his pants. I didn't know that was actually possible."

I don't respond. I don't trust myself to right now. I want to shake her for staying even one day in that building. But more than that, I want to kill him.

"Where are we going?" she asks, as Parker takes her bag and I practically shove her in the back of the car.

"Somewhere else," I grit out between my teeth. I know exactly where I'm taking her. It's secure, luxurious, and close enough to my home that I can see her whenever I want, without being actually inside my home.

I reach out and haul her into my lap, needing to keep her close, feel her warmth against me, her citrus scent teasing my nostrils as I tuck her head under my chin and stroke her hair.

I don't know how she's going to feel about being my next door neighbor, but I don't care. She's not staying in this deathtrap of a building with that scumsucking excuse for a landlord one second longer.

***

Keeley

I don't know what I was expecting when Caden shoved me into his town car and then cradled me like I was his most cherished possession, but it certainly wasn't this.

The building in front of me is a beautiful, artistic sculpture in glass and steel, and probably one of the most recognizable landmarks in the city. It's famous for homing some of the richest people in the world, let alone the country. It's where Caden Fox lives. Well, it's listed as his home address. Honestly, considering how much time he spends at the office, I consider it a storage facility for clean shirts and toothpaste, but whatever. Ostensibly, this is his home. And I'm not ready for this.

"I don't think I can do this," I tell him, backing away towards the car.

He frowns at me, his eyes almost black. "Do what? Sleep in a proper bed? In a building which actually meets regulations? I own the building, you know. No one's going to assault you here. I take a dim view of such things."

"Oh, yes, I've noticed," I say faintly. His display an hour ago was an unexpected insight into the man beneath the tailored clothes and overflowing bank account. A barely controlled force of nature. No wonder his company is so successful.

He raises an eyebrow. "Are you harboring some regret over what transpired earlier? Because I can assure you, I am not."

"Oh no, not at all. Wallis is an asshole. I wish someone had punched him out a long time ago. I wish I had."

He shakes his head. "So what's the problem?"

I shift my weight from one foot to the other. "I...I don't think I'm ready to move in with you."

This time both eyebrows go up. "Keeley, you have misread the situation entirely. Much as I enjoy your company, I am not ready for you to move in with me either."

For some reason, instead of relief, nausea rolls in my stomach. "You're not? I mean, of course you're not. But...why are we here? I mean, you do live here, don't you? I've seen your address on paperwork at the office."

His lips curve in the faintest of smiles, and my nipples tingle. I should be scared of him, especially after his display of temper earlier, but if let's be honest here. If I'd had the chance, I'd have pushed him up against the nearest wall and demanded he take my cherry right then and there. A guy defending my honor like that? Hands down, *the* sexiest thing I've ever seen in my life.

"I do live here. Now you do too. There's a vacant penthouse. You might as well use it until you can make more permanent arrangements." He stands back and gestures towards the door. "Shall we?"

My stomach flips and drops. More permanent arrangements? Something better than a penthouse in the Fox Building?

I cut off that train of thought before it can lead somewhere totally unhelpful and allow him to escort me into the lobby, a monument to polished marble and discreet security. The doormen are built like brownstones and are clearly capable of far more than carrying people's bags.

We step into the elevator, and he pushes a key into the console, then hit some combination of buttons that doesn't make sense. It takes me a minute to realize it's a passcode to the upper floors of the building.

"You'll have your own key," he says, as the elevator rises so smoothly I can barely feel the movement. "I should imagine you'll find the passcode easy enough to remember."

I flick him a curious look. "It's my birthday," I point out.

"I know," he replies, as the doors open, revealing a small hallway with a door to either side. I stare at him. He acts like it's the most normal thing in the world to have changed his elevator passcode to my birthday.

Because he must have changed it. There's no way that same six digit combination has come up any other time in his life. The odds against it are astronomical, and yet... I'm jumping to conclusions. It doesn't mean anything. How can it? I'm a broke virgin nobody, his flavor of the week, but only the week. This isn't going anywhere long-term. How can it? I'm his assistant, nothing more.

I must remember that. And yet...

I drag my focus back to the here and now as he points at one of the doors. "That's my place. Since we work together, you'll know when I'm home. If you need anything, let me know. If I'm not around, just call down to the front desk, and they'll be happy to help. Now, this is your place, until you decide otherwise."

He accompanies me to the other door and

produces a keycard, pushing it into the slot. The door opens, and he says something, but I'm not listening anymore. I'm too busy staring at the palace he's just told me is mine.

It's huge. And bright. Those are my first impressions. As my eyes adjust, I pick out the recessed lighting and spotlights scattered here and there across the ceiling. Stepping forward, my shoes sink into luxurious, thick carpet. Cream carpet, and I hurriedly tug off my shoes before moving further into the vast open space. Forty feet away, across three cream leather couches arranged in a U shape, floor to ceiling plate glass windows showcase the most spectacular view across the city. In the distance I can even see the goddamn ocean.

A massive TV, almost as big as the twin bed I left behind this evening, hangs on the wall, above a fireplace big enough to roast an ox in. Opposite, a kitchen space big enough to swallow my entire old apartment gleams, with a double wall oven, six burner stove, and an island with six stools ranged along it. Beyond that are a couple of doors, and there are more doors to my right and left, too. I have no idea where they lead, and I'm almost afraid to ask. This is too much. This is...Heaven.

A shadow falls across me, and I look up to see Caden frowning down at me. I open my mouth to say thank you, to say anything, but my mouth is already open and I can't produce words. I stare up at him and burst into tears.

I'm horribly embarrassed, and yet I can't stop crying. I knew places like this existed, but I had no idea I'd ever get to see inside one of them, let alone actually live there, and it's so completely opposite to the kinds of places I've been living in for the last five years that I can't adjust. I can't take it in. How is it possible for someone like me to live in a place like this?

Caden's arms come around me, and I collapse against him, my tears soaking into his shirt. He tenses for a moment, then sweeps me up and carries me...somewhere. I don't know where. All I know is that my world has been turned upside down again and again in the last week, and I've reached the end of my ability to cope with the constant change.

He sits down and cradles me against him, his arms warm and strong and solid around me, and I just cry and cry and cry until I run out of tears. He strokes my hair and my back, murmuring words I can't hear, but the cadence is soothing. Eventually the tears dry up, and I'm left breathless and shy, afraid to face him after falling apart so spectacularly.

"Better?" he asks quietly, after a long while, and I nod, still not keen on lifting my head and meeting his eyes. Naturally, he won't let me get away with that. He slides a long finger under my chin and lifts it until I have no choice but to meet his gaze. "Afraid to look at me, Keeley? Since when?"

I swallow, horribly aware of the heat of his touch burning my skin and the closeness and solidity of his body against mine. In spite of everything we've done in his car, somehow this feels far more intimate. Looking around, I notice the decor is different. We must be in his apartment now. And yet...

"Not afraid," I rasp, and I stop to clear my

throat. "Just embarrassed to have ruined your shirt with all that salt water."

He makes a small sound of amusement. "It's a shirt, not a wall hanging. Besides, that's what washers were invented for."

I smile faintly, and his lips curve in response.

"That's better." He strokes my hair, his hand settling at the back of my neck, the possessiveness of his touch making me sigh. I control the impulse to arch back into it. He's just being kind.

"I must apologize," he says, his thumb stroking over my throat, back and forth, back and forth.

"W-what for?" I stammer, barely able to focus through the haze of sensory overload brought on by that gentle contact. My skin prickles, electricity skittering down my spine. My nipples tingle, hardening in anticipation of his touch, and my clit throbs, desperate for contact.

"I should have realized how much pressure you've been under. I knew you were tired; it's why I left you alone in the car tonight, but I didn't factor in the other issues you've been dealing with in your personal life. For that, I am truly sorry. I've thrown a lot at you in the past few days, and you've handled it all admirably. I'm impressed with your strength."

I snort. "So strong, I completely fell apart."

"We all have our tipping points, Keeley. There's no shame in admitting that."

I draw in a deep breath, then let it out again. "I was in my freshman year of college when Dad passed away. I couldn't afford tuition on my own, so I dropped out. I sold his house and rented rooms here and there, but with no degree, it was hard to get decent jobs. I didn't want to spend the money left from selling his place, especially without a good job to fall back on when it finally ran out. When I met Jason, I thought eventually I'd be able to move out of that dump, get a nice place with him, just have a nicer life. I figured I could take evening classes, get my degree. But when he took my money..." I bite my lip. I haven't let myself face this since Jason left. I knew I'd fall apart if I did, and I just didn't have the luxury of that. "He took the contents of my savings account, too. All the money Dad left me, from the house sale, all of it, gone."

His arms lock around me, and his breathing intensifies as his eyes turn cold, menacing. Shit. I've pissed him off. I should have known better than to offload this on him. It's not his place to be comforting his employee anyway. I'm just his assistant. It's not like we're a couple or anything.

"I'm sorry," I mutter. "I shouldn't be telling you this. It's not your problem."

His face changes, and if I thought he looked mad before, now he looks downright murderous. I try to push away from him, but he easily holds me in place. The hand on the back of my neck fists in my hair, drawing my head back so that I'm forced to meet his gaze.

"Everything about you is my business, Keeley. Your problems are my problems. What exactly do you think is going on here? That this is just some kind of short-term fling? You think I touch all my assistants the way I touch you? You think I spread their legs and drink from their pussies until their screams echo around me? You think I fuck them all with my hands and mouth until they beg for mercy, and for more?"

The images pouring through my brain are beyond hot, and my body is burning up. I gasp for air, my lungs seizing with memories of him doing all those things to me, and of me enjoying every second of it, losing myself in the pleasure he gave me.

"I-I'm sorry," I gasp. "I've never done anything like this before. I don't know what's going on here. I just know that I want you, more than I've ever wanted anyone. But how can you want me the same way? I'm nobody."

His eyes narrow, glittering like stars. "You aren't nobody to me. You're *everything*."

Before I can process his words, his lips crash down on mine, his tongue sweeping into my mouth, obliterating conscious thought. I open for him, moaning as his lips and tongue dominate my mouth, possessing me, controlling me. Something dark and needy slides within me, and my hand fists in his shirt, trying to pull him closer.

His hand skims over my waist to cover my breast. Even through my shirt and bra, his touch burns, and I arch into him, desperate for more. My nipple pebbles, and even with two layers of fabric between his skin and mine, the friction is almost unbearable.

Suddenly, the exquisite pleasure of his tongue in my mouth, his hand on my breast, vanishes, and I force my eyes open, trying to figure out why he stopped.

He lifts me away from him, and the sting of rejection bites deep. I can't handle this. Not twice in one day. No, twice in mere *hours*. I can't—

"The bedroom's that way," he says, pointing. "Move."

I stare at him, and his eyes narrow. "I'm not taking your virginity on a fucking couch, Keeley. Get in the bedroom. *Now*."

My eyes widen as his voice lowers to little more than a growl. A growl that has moisture pooling in my pussy while my knees shake.

I turn, seeing a door with a brass handle, and I stagger towards it, reaching out to the wall to keep myself upright.

"Keep moving, Keeley," he says when I falter, wondering if I really want to do this. His voice decides me. Deeper than a lake at midnight, dark as chocolate, dangerous as a lion's den, it drives me forward. Awareness of him following me down the short passage keeps my feet moving, one step after another, until I turn the door handle to reveal the most enormous bed I've ever seen in my life.

It's seven feet wide, with pale sheets that gleam faintly in the light filtering in from the city beyond the floor to ceiling windows. I stop in the doorway, frozen by the sight of this massive bed, and the knowledge of what's about to happen.

Am I really okay with this?

"Keeley?" His voice behind me has me moving forwards, but my steps are jerky, halting. His hands touch my shoulders, and he turns me to face him. "Do you want this? Because it doesn't have to happen. You can go back to your penthouse, sleep alone. Your job will not be endangered by you choosing to walk away from me."

His eyes rove over my face. I can barely take in

what he's saying. Is he for real?

"Granted, I would probably assign you to one of the other executives. It would be too difficult to keep seeing you every day if I couldn't touch you, but you'd still have a job, and you'd keep your current salary." He leans in, and my heart skips, but instead of kissing me, his lips brush against my ear. "Just don't share your pay grade with anyone. You earn more than some of the executives."

I laugh. I can't help it. Caden joking is the last thing I expected in this situation, and the best possible thing he could have done. Just like that, my nerves melt away. "Really?" I ask, looking up at him.

"Of course." He pretends to frown, but I know what a real Caden Fox frown looks like. "Good executive assistants are hard to come by, as you should know."

Then the humor fades from his eyes, replaced by something hot and dark, something *predatory*, and the air locks up in my lungs. It takes me a moment to pick up on the fact that he's not moving. He's leaving the first step to me.

If I want this, I have to take it.

I step forward and rise up on my tiptoes to brush my lips over his. "Take me, Mr. Fox," I murmur against his mouth. "Please."

His eyes darken almost to black, and then he steps back. "Take off your skirt."

My mouth goes dry, and I lick my lips. His eyes track the movement, but I know what he wants me to do. I have my orders.

I reach behind me to slide down the zipper of my skirt, then shimmy it down over my hips, stepping out of the pool of fabric.

He nods. "Now the blouse."

My skin prickles, and I feel the cotton pulling at my sensitized skin as I take my time undoing each button. Eventually, I reach the last one and slide the material off my shoulders to fall to the floor, leaving me standing in front of him in my plain white cotton bra and panties.

His hands move to his pants, sliding down the zipper, easing the fabric down over his hips. As it falls, I see why he was so careful about taking them off. The bulge in his groin is huge, and I can't stop staring at it. How the hell is that going to fit?

"Let me take care of the details," he tells me, correctly interpreting my expression, as usual, before undoing the buttons on his shirt and shucking it behind him. Socks, shoes and underwear follow, until he's gloriously, magnificently naked.

"Breathe, Keeley," he says, and I do as I'm told. But it's hard. Like him. So hard. I drag my eyes away from his cock and find the rest of him is just as stunning. Broad shoulders tapering to a lean waist, every muscle chiseled as though from raw granite, from the heavy pecs to the ridged abs to the solid thighs. And then he moves.

He stalks towards me, and instinctively, I back away until the backs of my knees hit the bed, forcing me to sit down. He looms over me, and I crawl backwards over the mattress until I find myself pressed up against the headboard, with nowhere left to go. He covers my body with his, and the weight of him makes me arch, wanting more of that glorious pressure between my legs, desperate to ease the ache that's growing there.

He laces his fingers through mine and raises my hands above my head, pinning them to the pillow while his mouth descends to ravage mine. His hips flex, his cock sliding between my legs to rub over my cotton-covered core, making me moan and arch into him. I raise my legs to wrap them around his waist, trying to pull him closer, trying to force him into giving me more contact, more sensation, more *everything*.

I should know better by now.

He lifts himself off me, and I cry out at the loss of his heated skin and muscle against mine. But he doesn't care, simply reaches out and lifts a cuff from the side of the bed, fixing it around my ankle. The restraint makes me breathe faster, my breasts rising and falling as I drag in air, but he doesn't seem to notice. He merely turns and cuffs my other ankle, then lowers himself over me again. He presses my palms against the headboard, encouraging my fingers to curl around it, before resuming his leisurely torture of my senses.

This time, when I try to wrap my legs around his waist, I can't. I can bend my knees, but the clinking chain isn't long enough for anything more. I can only feel, his chest rubbing against my bra-covered breasts, the pressure combined with the friction of fabric over my nipples driving me mad, while his mouth controls my breathing, my gasps and moans of pleasure and desperation.

His palms skim my sides, heat rippling over my skin in the wake of his touch. His mouth trails down my throat as he pushes my bra aside to mold my breast, pinching my nipple, making me shriek even as I arch into his touch, begging for more.

He nips at the soft skin of my throat, and I gasp, then moan as he soothes the sting with his tongue before licking his way south. It's getting harder to keep my hands on the headboard. I want to touch him, tunnel my hands into his hair, wrap myself around him. The delicate chains rattle as his mouth closes over my breast and I groan in frustration as I angle my hips, desperate to draw him closer to me. Every touch of his mouth on my skin, his hands shaping my flesh, sends molten lava rolling through me, electric storms dancing in my blood. My pussy clenches, aching, *needing*, and yet his delicious weight is always just to one side or the other, and there isn't a damn thing I can do about it.

The knowledge makes me writhe beneath him, the awareness that he controls me, my body, my pleasure, that I'm utterly in his hands, driving me higher as my clit tingles with every flick of his fingers over my nipple, every lick of his tongue over my quivering flesh.

His mouth moves lower, leaving a hot, wet trail down my belly while his hands skim down my thighs, his fingers brushing over my skin, making me squirm. I want him so badly, my body is oversensitive to his touch, every graze of his skin on mine making me jerk against the headboard, against my restraints.

He looks up at me, his mouth hovering over my wet, heated core. I don't know what he's waiting for, but I daren't say a word. I want to beg, to plead, to grab his head and push it right where I want it, but I don't do any of those things. I only watch him watching me, biting my lip so as not to speak, and after an eternity of waiting, pinned beneath that sapphire stare, his lips curve.

"Good girl," he says. "Now for your reward." One quick yank, and my panties disappear, torn to shreds.

I have no time to react before his tongue slicks into my pussy, thrusting deep, and I arch off the bed at the hot slide of his flesh within mine. He parts me with his hand and licks me from asshole to clit, one long, hot, tortuous stroke, then slides two fingers inside me while his lips envelop my clit, nipping and nibbling, sucking and licking.

I can't breathe, can't make a sound. There's no air. My body is locked in one long, trembling arc of sensation. Then an orgasm tears me apart, and I wail my pleasure to the four walls as I come and come and come against his hands and mouth.

Even as I'm coming apart around him, he continues to caress me, to stroke and lick, to thrust and tease, and the pleasure continues to build. It's too much, and I beg him to stop, but he doesn't, and another orgasm rips through me, followed almost immediately by another.

My body clenches and releases, clenches and releases, dragging me through hoop after hoop of pleasure. Caden clearly knows my body far better than I do, as he finally allows me some respite, his fingers sliding out of my body. He leans over me, and presses his wet fingers to my lips. Instinct takes over and my tongue wraps around his fingers, tasting my musk and the salty tang of his skin mixed together. It's a heady aroma, and I arch beneath him, unbearably turned on by the scent and the taste, both reminding me of the pleasure he just brought me, and suddenly, I'm desperate for more. I want him inside me. I want *everything*.

He kneels between my legs, reaching back to cup my ankle in his large hands. Something clicks and the cuff falls away. A moment later, my other ankle is also released, but when he places my feet flat on the bed, I keep them there, and he smiles with approval.

Then he moves up my body, his weight settling between my thighs, and I watch, my breath getting shallow again. His cock slides through the wet curls at my core, grazing my clit, making me buck against him. He tunnels a hand into my hair and lifts my head so that he can lick and suck on my neck, teeth nipping at the sensitive flesh. I moan helplessly as I let go of the headboard to give him more access but spread my arms wide across the mattress. I won't touch him until he specifically tells me I may. He controls me without a single cuff or chain, and the knowledge has my head falling back as I gasp at his touch, the way he dominates me without a word.

His hips flex, his cock sliding back and forth between my legs, and it gets harder to breathe. I bite my lip to hold back the pleas building in my throat, and I'm rewarded when his hand covers my breast, plucking at my hardened nipple, sending a shot of pure pleasure spiking through me, straight from my nipple to my clit. I writhe against him, desperate for more and equally desperate for respite. This is torture. I can't survive it, no one could, and yet he continues to lick and nip and suck, his cock continuing its maddening rhythm between my legs, slicing against my soaked and swollen pussy until I'm on the point of bursting into flames. And then he changes the angle of his hips, and his cock slides into me in one long, deep, *hard* stroke, and I scream as pleasure and pain rock my body.

I sob for air, and but there's none to be had. He's buried so far inside me that I can feel him when I breathe, or try to. He fills me completely and I can't feel anything else. Can't see or hear anything but him, filling me, surrounding me, controlling me, like he has since the very first moment I met him.

"Okay?" he asks, brushing a strand of hair off my face. I nod, the pain already but a memory, then gasp as even that small movement sets off a string of tiny fires inside me as his cock rubs against the walls of my pussy. "Words, Keeley. I need you to say it."

"I'm okay." The words shudder out of me, but it doesn't matter, because then he starts to move and drives the world away, so that it's just him and me and the tsunami of sensation cascading through me with every thrust.

I want to hold him, but I daren't. My shoulders and thighs are screaming with the effort of holding back, and every sound out of my mouth is a shriek.

I arch and moan and gasp beneath him, and when he lowers his mouth to brush down the side of my neck, the delicate brush of sensation has me on the point of orgasm in less than a heartbeat.

"You may touch me," he mutters, his voice hard, and the power of it has my pussy starting to spasm.

The moment I lift my legs to wrap around his hips, the change in angle has him hitting an entirely new spot within me, and my orgasm shatters me into a thousand pieces of starglass. I can't stop screaming, but he doesn't stop moving, and another orgasm rips through me on the heels of the first, followed immediately by another. Wave after wave of pleasure rocks me, clenching me in a fist and throwing me over cliff after cliff, breaking me again and again until finally I'm nothing but stardust, floating through an eternal sky.

It feels like a long time later that I come back to myself, curled into his side, his arms around me as my head rests on his chest. I can't remember the last time I was this relaxed. I snuggle closer, and his arm tightens around me.

"Sleep, Keeley."

I smile against the bare skin of his chest, and try to reply, but I don't have the energy, and soon after I drift away into a dark and dreamless sleep.

***

Keeley

I wake up to an empty bed, and that sting of rejection turns my stomach. I sniff, determined to maintain some kind of professional demeanor if he is, but then a distinctive aroma has me sitting up in bed. I wince, last night's activities making themselves felt in the form of aches in places I didn't know I had, but the smell of bacon is too distracting to ignore.

I scramble out of bed, grabbing one of Caden's shirts when I can't find my own clothes. I reach for the door, and jump back as it opens before I can touch the handle. Caden's eyes sweep over me, darkening in a way that's becoming highly familiar.

"You'd better come out for breakfast," he growls. "If I come in there, we won't leave before midday."

That doesn't sound so bad, and I'm about to say so when my stomach snarls. I grimace with embarrassment, but he just smiles and gestures towards the living area.

"Sorry," I mutter as I pass him, then gasp in shock as he grabs me and presses me up against the wall. He's only wearing a pair of sweats, the most casual by far that I've ever seen him, and all that bare, hard muscle pressing up against me is enough to scramble my brains. My hands land on his shoulders, but I can't resist sliding them down to luxuriate in the feel of rippling muscle. His hands catch mine and lift them above my head, and even that small restraint has me melting against him.

"Don't ever apologize for being human, Keeley. We both burned a hell of a lot of calories last night, and it was your first time. You need to eat, and it's my pleasure to feed you."

The way his lips and tongue curl around the word 'pleasure' has heat trickling through me once more, and the way his eyes glitter tells me he's not unaffected either. I flex my hips against him, and he groans.

"Minx," he growls, before lowering his mouth to mine and kissing me, his tongue and lips reminding me exactly who's in charge here. Desire has my nipples tightening, dark and needy moans falling from my lips. I'm only too aware of the hardening bulge pressing against my belly, but when he lifts his head, he simply steps away from me and gestures towards the source of the breakfast smell.

It turns out to be a hell of a lot more than bacon. Eggs, sausage, hash browns, oatmeal, toast, about ten different kinds of cereal... I look up at him, completely bemused, and rather entertained to see him looking embarrassed.

"I don't know what you like for breakfast," he admits, as though caught out doing something supremely un-billionaire-like. "So I just told the kitchen to send some of everything."

Something melts in my chest, and I step into him and wrap my arms around his waist. "That's possibly the sweetest thing a man's ever done for me."

He raises his eyebrows, but puts his arms around me as I hug him. "You have very low standards," he says, his deep voice vibrating through me. "I'm going to work on raising them."

His gravel mixer voice makes me close my eyes, reveling in the feeling of being near him. It's some of the least sexual contact we've ever had, and yet somehow, it ties us even tighter together. I'm starting to feel like there's more here than just as fling. Maybe there's more to this than I thought. Something in his voice certainly has me intrigued.

"How do you plan on doing that?" I ask, as I sit down and help myself to bacon and hash browns.

He sits down and serves himself, not meeting my eye for so long, I start to get nervous.

"Caden, what's going on?"

Finally, he looks up at me. "There's a fundraising gala tomorrow night. They're deathly boring, and I have to go since my company is a major sponsor of the organization holding the event. I would very much like it if you would attend with me."

Now it's my turn to raise an eyebrow. "You're asking? I mean, instead of just telling me?"

His eyes narrow, and his jaw clenches, and I'm confused. He takes a sip of coffee before responding.

"Keeley, I very much enjoy being in control of almost every aspect of my life, and yes, that extends to the bedroom. But I have no wish to control you outside of that. You have your own life, with your own needs. I want to look after you, show you off, bring you as far into my life as you will allow, but I understand that your life is very different, and I'm not about to order you to do anything you're not comfortable with."

I consider his words. On the surface, they're incredibly sweet, but I get the feeling there's something he's not telling me. "Why wouldn't I be comfortable at this event?"

He snorts. "Everyone there is fake. Fake smiles, fake sincerity, fake small talk. Well, there are the odd exceptions, but they are few and far between. You, on the other hand, are real. Genuine. You wear your emotions right out in the open for anyone to see. It's refreshing, but not everyone will see it as the gift I do."

I read between the lines. "They'll be catty behind my back because I'm not rich and a size two?"

He grins, and I'm struck speechless. It's possibly the first genuine smile I've seen on his face, and it takes my breath away.

"Pretty much," he acknowledges with a tip of his head.

I shrug. "Sounds just like high school. I survived four years of that. I can survive, what, four hours of some fancy shindig? Oh shit." I drop my fork as the huge hole in Caden's grand plan to show me off hits me.

"What?" He looks genuinely concerned. "What is it?"

"I'm really sorry, but I haven't got anything even remotely appropriate to wear."

He sits back in his chair with a sigh of relief. "For a minute there, I thought there was a real problem. I know you don't own anything you could wear there. That's why we're going shopping."

Part of me, a very small part, is insulted beyond measure that he just assumed I don't have any really nice dresses. I mean, obviously I don't, but he didn't have to assume.

Most of me, however, is very happy at the idea of going shopping. I've got money in the bank, although... "How much is my rent?"

He stares at me like he has no idea what I'm talking about.

"My rent, Caden. For the place next door."

His brows draw together in confusion. "There's no rent. Consider it a perk of the job."

"No rent? Caden, you can't be serious. I have to pay rent." He opens his mouth to say something stupid and I hold up a hand to forestall him. "No,

I'm serious. I pay my way. I always have, and I'm not about to stop now."

I manage to stop myself from stating my true issue; I refuse to be a kept woman, and if I don't pay rent, that's exactly what I'd be. I have a feeling saying that wouldn't be productive at this point, though, so I keep it to myself.

His jaw works for a minute, until finally, he sighs. "Fine. Rent is one dollar a month. Take it or leave it."

I gape at him, desperately wanting to argue the point, yet horribly aware I won't get anywhere. All I can do is give in.

At least it'll leave me plenty spare for clothes shopping.

***

Keeley

I should have known better. We've been shopping for four hours, and Caden has flatly refused to allow me to pay for anything. That said, at one point I actually saw the label in something the personal shopper was about to drop over my head and gulped.

Vera Wang is substantially above my pay grade, even with my new job.

The pile of dresses and outfits is growing, although I'm speaking metaphorically, since we're not actually carrying anything. It'll all be sent to Caden's place. Evidently they have his address on file, as well as his credit card details.

I'm becoming increasingly uncomfortable with

the amount of money he's spending on me. I want to believe this is a long-term arrangement, but this feels like too much, too soon. He hasn't said a word about any kind of relationship, and I'm for damn sure not going to mention it. I figure, if I don't say anything about it, I can avoid thinking about it, too.

There's nothing worse than getting your hopes up only to have them ripped away.

My resolve lasts as long as it takes for the personal shopper at the third store to appear with a stunningly gorgeous dress, all emerald green satin and lace. I almost cry when I see it, and when she puts it on me and I see myself in the mirror, I actually do shed a tear, and then another, because this is the most beautiful dress in the world, and I can't bear to think of a time when I won't be able to wear it.

Obviously, when it ends with Caden, I won't be taking any of this stuff with me. I'm not here for the clothes.

"What's wrong?" he asks, when I finally make it out into the little private viewing area, still brushing tears away from under my eyes. He stands up, prowling over to me to take my hands and brush away another stray tear. "You look beautiful."

"It's the most gorgeous dress I've ever seen," I agree.

He shakes his head, his smile fading. "You're the most beautiful woman I've ever seen. All this, all these things we're getting, they're just attempts to do you justice."

My heart does a funny little skip in my chest. I tell it to stop dancing, they're just words. But I can't help feeling like maybe, just maybe, this isn't just a few days or weeks. Maybe it could be something else. Something real.

His phone beeps as I turn to head back into the changing area, but I turn back when I hear him swear. "What's wrong?"

He shakes his head. "The Dayton paperwork. Triskelion are asking about it and I don't remember signing it." He raises his head, looking genuinely upset. "I'm really sorry, sweetheart, I'm going to have to go back into the office. It must still be on my desk."

I smile and laugh. "No, it isn't. You signed it on Thursday. It was with a bunch of other things I sent out with the courier that afternoon. Henry called to confirm receipt just before we left. Triskelion should have it back by Monday, but they can call Henry to ask him where he's at with it."

He stares at me for so long, that I start to feel subconscious. "What?"

He smiles, a gentle, genuine smile, and I melt a little more. "Beautiful, intelligent, and organized. You really are perfect."

He backs me up towards the changing room, his intentions clear in his eyes. I want to laugh for the sheer pleasure of it, but the sound lodges in my throat, swamped by a wave of heat that rushes through me.

"We can't," I murmur, as he pushes me through the curtain, his hands hot and strong on my shoulders.

"Why not?"

Staring at him, I can barely breathe, let alone string a sentence together. "We might damage the dress."

He pauses, searching my face. I don't know what he's looking for, but he seems satisfied, because eventually he nods. "In that case, I'd better practice taking it off, hadn't I?"

***

Keeley

The gala is about ten times more glitzy than I expected, and a hundred times more intimidating. Everywhere I look, women are wearing dresses that even I, with my minimal knowledge of fashion, can see are worth more than I'll make in a year, even at the extremely generous salary Caden is paying me. The way their eyes slide over me, dismissing me, gets my back up, though.

Having a shitton of money in the bank doesn't mean you have class, and it shows. I force myself not to cling to Caden's arm, but he's great about keeping me by him as much as he can. Especially when women are clearly trying to get his attention.

The first one to stroll up looks at Caden like she wants to eat him, greeting him with a throaty, "Caden, darling, how *are* you?"

My hackles rise at her tone, even as her eyes flick over me and then away, clearly writing me off as unimportant. I open my mouth to say something, but Caden's arm around my waist forestalls whatever was about to come out of my mouth, which is probably a good thing.

"We're very well, Marie, thank you very much. Marie, I don't believe you've met my girlfriend,

Keeley Gant. Keeley, this is Marie Bolton. She's married to Henry Bolton. Where is Henry, by the way?"

I bite my lip in an effort to hide a smile. Marie looks like she just swallowed a lemon when Caden calls me his girlfriend. I must admit, it gives me a warm fuzzy feeling to hear him acknowledge there's something between us in public like that.

But she actually turns a bit green when he asks about her husband. It has to be as pointed a way as possible in this level of society to tell someone you're not interested. I'll give her props for a quick recovery, though. It only takes her a second to get her breath back, and then she's all smiles.

"He's around," she says. "Which reminds me, I should really go and find him."

"You do that," says Caden, as she stalks away from us. He looks down at me. "How are you enjoying the party?"

I grimace, then feel small. It's a stunning event. There has to be enough money in this room to pay off the national debt. Most of the girls I've known in my life would give their eye teeth to be here, and on the arm of one of the most, if not *the most*, gorgeous guy in the room. It's just so not me.

"It's very nice," I tell him, but it sounds lame even to my ears. I risk glancing up at him, expecting to see his jaw tighten and those eyes turn dark, and not in a good way. He hates it when I lie, and even more when he knows I'm saying what I think he wants to hear.

Instead, he shocks me, and evidently half the room, by throwing his head back and laughing. Heads turn, eyebrows rise, but he doesn't seem to care. He leans down to whisper in my ear, and I suppress the shiver that runs down my spine as his breath tickles my skin.

"I don't like them either, but at least the Marie Boltons of this world will back off for a while, since I'm out with my girlfriend."

Heat unfurls in my chest at his casual use of the g-word, and I drag my thoughts together. "She seemed really surprised."

He smiles down at me, a few inches taller even with me wearing four inch spike heels. "She'll get over it."

A number of other women approach at various intervals, and each time, he pins me firmly to his side and introduces me very politely as his girlfriend before sending them away to talk to someone else.

The men generally talk over me, but Caden makes every effort to involve me in their conversations. Years of reading the financial pages with my dad, then running calendars and correspondence for a variety of corporate executives, have left me with a fairly solid understanding of business, and it's gratifying to see them do a double take when they realize I actually have something to contribute. Caden's careful protectiveness is such that by the time I need to visit the bathroom, I'm not worried about navigating this huge space and all these strangers by myself.

They're just people. No more nor less than I am.

Heading back into the ballroom, a man steps into my path. I vaguely remember him from earlier in the evening, talking to one of the many women

Caden has brushed off tonight.

"Keeley, is it?" His smile is too wide, too bright, and I automatically distrust him. "Jake Huntmeyer."

He holds out his hand, and good manners dictate that I shake, even though I don't want to touch any part of this sleazy guy. He keeps a hold of my hand far longer than he should, and something cold and hard settles in my belly.

"I should really be rejoining Caden," I tell him, adding, "my boyfriend." Just in case he's managed to miss that fact.

He smiles, but it's not friendly, more pitying. "Yes, I heard he had made it very clear you were his. Most undignified. Might as well have pissed on you, really. Not that it will last."

My righteous indignation at being waylaid fades away. "What do you mean?"

He gives me a condescending look. "My dear girl, you are a very attractive woman, but Caden Fox is a man of many and varied tastes. Why do you think he has a different woman on his arm at every single event he attends? He's easily bored. His focus is legendary, I'll admit, and I have no doubt that he's paying you the... *proper attention*, shall we say? But it will end, and when it does, please do call me. My attention is not nearly as fickle, and I promise you will find me more than generous." He pulls a card out of his breast pocket and hands it to me. Cold fury and fear war within me, keeping me nailed to the spot long enough for him to put the card in my hand. "It was a pleasure meeting you, Keeley."

The way his voice lingers over my name makes

me want to take a shower, and I snap back to myself, send him a furious glare, then turn away, dropping his card into the nearest pot plant as I storm past, scanning the gathering desperately in search of Caden.

When I see him, I actually feel tears burn the back of my eyes, and I blink them back and take a few deep breaths before stepping up next to him. That warm smile I'm starting to get used to lights up his face, but then it fades.

"What's wrong?" he murmurs in my ear. Max is only a couple of feet away, suddenly pretending to be very interested in the ceiling, but I know he can hear us, and I also know I don't want a scene. Caden would not be impressed by what just happened, and now that I'm with him, the chill in my gut soon disperses.

"Nothing," I tell him. "I just couldn't find you for a minute. I thought I'd lost you."

The heat I'm becoming more and more familiar with rises in his eyes. "You're never getting rid of me," he says quietly, and the pressure in my chest eases. I smile up at him, although the fear isn't totally gone.

I need to enjoy every possible minute I can with this man. It won't last forever. It can't. I don't fit in his world, and he'd never fit in mine. I need to remember how to look after myself. The last thing I need is to fall prey to yet another asshole once this is over, and it seems like the vultures are already circling.

I really know how to attract the bastards.

I slide my hand around his waist and feel him relax against me. He catches my hand in his and kisses my fingers before pulling me against him again.

A minute later, he looks down at me. "Would you like a drink? I'm so sorry, darling. I was so caught up, I completely forgot to ask."

I flick an apologetic glance towards Max. "It's okay. I wouldn't want to interrupt."

His brows draw together with annoyance. "You're not interrupting. I interrupted to ask if you'd like a drink."

Pinned by his gaze, I figure it's safest to opt for honesty. "Okay. I'd love an orange juice."

"You'll be okay here with Max?"

"I'll protect her with my life," says Max, in a casual, offhand way which nonetheless makes me think he's totally serious. Caden's gaze, however, doesn't waver from my face.

"I'll be fine," I tell him, and he brushes his lips over mine before disappearing into the crowds.

There's a moment's silence. I have no idea what to talk to Max about. I know a fair bit about business, but I can't think of anything new to add to the conversation. I'm just starting to feel uncomfortable when he makes the decision for me.

"I've never seen him so solicitous of a woman's wellbeing," he says. "Well, anyone's wellbeing, actually."

I raise an eyebrow at him. "Really?"

"Oh, indeed. Nor, for that matter, have I ever seen him so relaxed." Max looks down at me, and he seems like a completely different person.

Gone is the carefree, always smiling Max I've come to quite like over the past week or so. In his place stands a quiet, serious man with calculating eyes. This is Max the businessman. The laughter and devil-may-care attitude is just a mask. I shiver. I'd hate to cross Max in business. Or any other way, for that matter.

"It's like he's finally seeing something in life worth enjoying other than making money. I must admit to being a little jealous." says Max, sipping his glass of whiskey. His lips curve, just slightly. "You're good for him. Keep it up."

I stare at him, wanting him to elaborate. As far as I can see, all Caden gets from me is sex, and realistically speaking, he could get that from any woman in this room, even the married ones.

Maybe especially the married ones.

He doesn't seem interested in saying anything more on the subject, and I turn to look for Caden. Ice water trickles inside me when in spot him, his head bowed to hear what a tall, slim blonde inside murmuring inside his ear. She steps back, all smiles, and he smiles back. A genuine, Caden Fox panty-melting smile.

I thought inside was the only one who got those smiles. He sees me and his smile widens as he hurries towards me. I try to fake a decent smile in response, but I have to turn to face Max instead, pretending he just said something. Caden always knows when I'm faking, and I can't have this out with him right now.

My skin prickles like it always does when he's near, so that I don't jump when he reappears, holding out my orange juice. He kisses me again, then laces his fingers through mine to hold me close by his side before resuming his conversation. I sip my orange juice and relish the heat and strength of his body pressed up against mine, and I try not to cry. I don't fit in his world, no matter what Max says. That idiot Huntmeyer was right about one thing. I can't survive here on my own. When Caden decides to move on, I'll be alone.

Again.

Even worse, it looks like he's chosen his next flavor. He's already leaving.

But not yet. For now, he's mine and I'm his. I press closer to him, hoping to draw comfort from his nearness, and pretend that the pressure of his hand on my hip is enough to drive away the fear.

***

Keeley

It's late when the other shoe finally drops. Caden and Max and I are standing with a couple of other guys, talking about a big merger that's been rumored, when another man joins the group. He's shorter than the others, and rounder, but he has an air of authority about him, and he's immediately allowed into the group. His face lights up when he sees me, but I have to force myself not to recoil when he holds out his hand. There's something about him that makes me nervous. His eyes are hard, calculating, and he looks at me with an expression bordering on avarice.

"Fox," he says, as I shake his hand and he lifts my hand to his wet lips. "You always associate with the most beautiful women. Where did you find this lovely specimen?"

Caden laughs, a dark sound masquerading as

humor, and pulls my hand away from the newcomer's grasping fingers under the pretext of brushing his own lips over my skin. "Horsden, stop kissing my woman. This is Keeley, my most recent assistant."

Shock freezes me in place. He's had his hands on me all evening, except for my unfortunately excursion to the bathroom, but this the first time he's referred to me as his assistant. To everyone else, I was his girlfriend. What's changed?

That woman, the blonde I saw him with. He no longer considers me his girlfriend, because he's already found the next woman to warm his bed.

I've been wondering what I am to him, hoping I'm special, that I haven't given up everything to yet another man who'll cast me aside as soon as he's got what he wants.

But no. I'm his assistant.

Horsden's eyes narrow, and I force my face into a pleasant expression. This is a man who thrives on seeing others squirm, who likes to twist the knife. Not someone to show your weaknesses to.

I force myself to listen to what Caden's saying. I can't get away right now. It would look too obvious. And even if I did, where would I go? My only home now is right opposite Caden's, and I can't stay there.

Oh God, my job.

I drag my thoughts out of their death spiral into panic, and focus.

"I'd be lost without her," he's saying, and I feel a faint wisp of hope unfurl inside. Maybe, just maybe, I'm overreacting. This isn't the end.

Horsden laughs. "Well, you'll have to do

without her eventually, won't you? You don't hold on to them for long."

Caden sighs. "Yes, I suppose so. All good things must come to an end. Isn't that right, darling?"

He turns and looks down at me, and I tamp down on the nausea rolling in my belly, forcing myself to smile a smile that will fool even him.

I was wrong. I was so, *so* wrong.

I stand and make small talk for a few minutes, doing my best to avoid Horsden's knowing gaze. There's something about the look on his face that reminds me of the guy who stopped me outside the bathroom earlier. It seems Caden's world is full of predators, and not just the corporate kind.

I can't stay here. I can't stand here with his arm around my waist, knowing he's already put an expiration date on our relationship. Hell, at this point I have to be honest with myself. It's not a relationship. It never was. It was just sex. Really hot sex, but still just sex.

And some really tender moments. That I now have to try and forget, because I can walk away from good sex, however much it hurts.

I don't know if I can walk away from a heartbreak.

So I won't. I excuse myself and pretend to head for the bathroom, telling myself it's not love, it never was. I can't love someone who can't commit to me, and let's face it, Caden can't even commit to a lunch choice. Even his towncar is a different model every day.

Variety is the spice of life, indeed.

I should be grateful I lasted a week.

A hysterical laugh bubbles up in my throat, and

I bite down on it, and my tongue. I am grateful. Grateful for a well-paid job, a massive salary boost, and some really amazing orgasms. I want to count the clothes on that list, but I know I won't take them with me. It would feel too much like I'd prostituted myself, and I can't handle that, not on top of everything else.

Unless I sell them to make rent somewhere, but that will take time, and I have to leave Caden tonight. And his glorious spare penthouse.

What was I thinking, letting him move me in there?

I collect my coat from the cloakroom near the main entrance, and then stand there, staring out at the street.

What do I do now? And where the hell do I go?

***

Caden

Keeley only went to the bathroom a couple of minutes ago, but I miss her already. The sweet warmth of her soft curves against my side has made this evening almost fun, and definitely tolerable, even if imagining all the things I'll do to her when we get home has rendered the whole evening a kind of delicious torture.

I sip my whiskey, only half listening to Horsden as he lists the attributes of what sounds like a very unappetizing investment prospect. I don't have much time for the man. He makes my skin crawl, but every now and then, he picks a winner, and my business brain insists I at least hear him out.

I'm disinclined to lend him a red cent at the moment. I didn't like the way he looked at Keeley, as though he'd already earmarked her for himself. His comments were aimed at making her feel like a temporary fixture, I know, and I can only hope she knows me well enough by now to know that I want her around for a lot longer than a few weeks, which has, up until now, been my usual maximum for any particular companion.

Keeley's different. She doesn't hang off me like Spanish moss, she's not constantly angling for expensive gifts, she's damn good at her job, and she can carry on a conversation about high finance with some of the most successful businessmen in the city. I don't know how I got by without her in charge of my office, but looking back, I can see that I was really just marking time until she showed up.

I frown at my watch. I didn't make a note of the time when she vanished to go to the bathroom, but I'm sure she's been gone longer than she should have been. I turn and scan the ballroom. It's starting to empty out now, but I can't see her anywhere. Her dress is like a traffic light, and the deep, emerald green should stand out like a beacon, but it's nowhere to be seen. A trickle of foreboding shivers down between my shoulder blades.

"Looking for your latest bit, Fox? I think I saw her headed for the main entrance. That must be the first time I've seen one of your...friends leaving without you. Maybe she joined Huntmeyer."

I know he's goading me, and one look at his face confirms it. He can't even hide his glee. I can barely recall anyone called Huntmeyer, though. *Who the hell is – ?*

"Jake Huntmeyer," Horsden supplies, clearly enjoying every second of my discomfiture. "I saw them talking before, hidden away near the powder rooms."

And then it all makes sense. I'd known Keeley was unhappy when she returned from her previous visit to the bathroom. I fix Horsden with a glare that's terrified many a bloated executive into compliance. The smirk fades from his face as he comprehends I'm not falling for his bullshit.

"So another man makes my girlfriend uncomfortable, to the point where she feels she has to leave, and you think that's entertaining?"

"They looked very cozy..." He trails off as the full weight of my murderous stare crushes him.

"Where is Huntmeyer?" I grit out.

"He left about an hour ago," says Max, who has been watching our altercation with an air of utmost disinterest. It's all a front. Max is one of the most intensely focused people I've ever met in my life. He cultivates the air of a devil-may-care playboy, but you don't become one of the wealthiest venture capitalists in the world by the age of thirty-five without the killing instinct of a tiger shark. Very few people recognize the look he gets when he's about to make his move, but he's wearing it now, and it's aimed purely at Horsden.

"He was alone," Max adds, even though we both know that means nothing. You'd have to be very stupid to leave an event with my date, and from what little I recall of Huntmeyer, he's not *that* stupid. I nod, pulling my phone out of my pocket and placing a call to Parker.

"I'll see you tomorrow," I tell Max as I wait for Parker to pick up. Max nods. We spar every morning in the basement of my building. It's how I discovered his killer instinct in the first place.

Parker picks up. "Sir?"

"I need to see one Jake Huntmeyer. Now."

"Sir." He hangs up, and I snatch my coat from the cloakroom attendant as I head out the door.

She left me. She actually left me. For Jake Huntmeyer? It seems uncharacteristic, and I don't really believe it, but I have to check with the man anyway. And possibly instill in him an awareness of the correct way to behave around my woman.

Parker arrives thirty seconds later, and I climb into the back. "You find Huntmeyer?" I ask.

"On our way there now, sir."

***

Caden

It doesn't take long to find out Huntmeyer doesn't have a clue where Keeley is. I grimace as I get back into the car, even as I shake out my hand. Punching him was possibly a bad idea, but accusing my girlfriend of leading him on when I knew for a fact she was very upset when she returned to me was an even worse one. At least I finally got the truth out of him. I could kill Horsden, but I have bigger problems right now.

"Where to now, sir?"

That's a good question. I blow out a breath. Where indeed? She's not with Huntmeyer... "Home."

My phone rings as the car pulls away from the curb, and I snatch it up, hope unfurling in my chest, only to crash into the pit of my stomach a moment later when I recognize Max's name on the caller ID. For a long moment I debate not picking up. Fear is a live thing, skittering up and down my spine, digging its claws into my gut. What if something's happened to her? What if she needs to speak to me but can't get through because I'm yapping to Max. Eventually, I sigh. There's call waiting, and Max is my oldest friend.

"Fox," I snap as I pick up the call.

"What the hell is going on with you?" Max wastes no time on small talk. "You shot out of here like you'd heard it was raining diamonds on Fifth Avenue."

"I can't find Keeley," I snarl, still angry at myself for not missing her sooner, but more angry at her for vanishing in the first place. Who pulls this kind of stunt? If she was upset, she only had to tell me. I'd have taken her home in a heartbeat and made her forget whatever the problem was before we were even halfway there. "She just walked out, and I don't know where she is."

There's complete silence on Max's end, to the point that I look at the phone to check the call is still connected. "Hello?"

"Yeah, I'm here," he says, sounding confused. "I hate to ask the obvious question, but it seems like I have to. I know you like the girl but, why is this a problem?"

"What? Of course it's a problem. She walked away from me, and I have no idea why, and I can't find her to ask!"

"Yes," he replies patiently, too patiently for my rapidly declining mood. "But why do you care? I distinctly remember you telling me, two or three girls ago, that you wished they'd just understand when things had run their course and walk away with some dignity."

"She's not—" I bite back the animalistic roar erupting from my mouth and force myself to calm down, just a little. Max is right. In the past, this was exactly how I would have wanted a liaison to end. But Keeley's not a liaison. She's... "She's not one of them. She's brilliant, so intelligent, and her knowledge of business is really quite astonishing, particularly in one so young, and with barely any college education. She's organized and beautiful, but also shy. When she looks at me, she sees me, not my money, not my company. She's not afraid to call me out on my bullshit, but she does it with grace. She's not like the others. She makes me want to live a life outside of the company, and I want to live it with her."

Another long silence. "For fuck's sake, Max, either say something or get off the goddamned line."

"I'll get off the goddamned line, then, but just think about this: everything you just told me, have you told her?"

The line goes dead, and I'm left staring at the phone. Trying to sort through the ragged bundle of emotions currently racing through me is not an efficient use of my time right now, so I simply hit the intercom and give Parker another address.

***

Caden

All the way over to Keeley's previous home, I've been praying she wasn't there, but as I leap out of the car, while it's still moving, I can't help hoping she is here after all.

I'm well aware that makes me a terrible person. The place is a deathtrap, and that's without factoring in the putrid excuse for a bottom-feeder of a landlord. I take the stairs three at a time and pound on the door of her old apartment.

"Keeley!" I roar, well aware she must be able to hear me through the door. If it's built to the same standard as the rest of the building, it's as thin as a verbal contract. I keep pounding until the door flies open, but it's not Keeley glaring at me across the threshold.

"Who the fuck is Keeley?" snaps a skinny guy in his twenties. He looks like he's never seen a gym in his life and is wearing a pair of threadbare TweetyPie boxers. As he takes me in, his aggressive stance wilts, and he closes the door a few inches.

"She used to live here," I growl, slamming my palm against the door to keep it open. "You know her?"

He shakes his head like a dog trying to get water out of its ear. "No, man. I-I just moved in today. I ain't never heard of no Keeley."

I narrow my eyes at him before pushing him aside and striding through the tiny studio apartment. Sadly, the kid's telling the truth. I grimace, but I'm in no mood to apologize. "Where's the landlord?"

"Uh, he's got a place on the first floor. I think he's got a girl in there, though..."

It's the wrong thing to say. I race down the stairs like the building's on fire, and as I reach the lobby, a young woman with a black eye presses herself back against the wall to avoid me.

"The landlord," I snap. "Where is he?"

She points a quivering finger at a door hidden in the shadows, and I thank her before turning to pound on the door. If Keeley's in the building, she's behind this door, and the anger in my gut tightens to pure rage. How could she? How could she leave me for this...this *scum*?

The door opens, and Wallis Jackson doesn't even get the chance to speak before I grab him by the front of his motheaten shirt and haul him up to eye level. "Where is she?"

"Where's who—"

I slam him against the wall. "You know who! Where is she?"

He shakes his head as tears roll down his face. This pathetic shred of roadkill is actually crying. "I don't know! Last I saw her, she was leaving with you."

I glare at him, unwilling to believe him, but a quick search of his squalid apartment reveals he's telling the truth. I storm out, but as I head through the lobby, his snide voice reaches me.

"You should keep better track of her, man, not that she's worth it. That one's a whore, through and through."

This time, when I get back in the car, I'm grateful for the ice in the champagne bucket. My hand stings like a bitch.

I let my head fall back against the seat as the ice quickly turns my bruised knuckles numb.

Where the hell is she? And when I find her, how am I going to convince her she should stay with me?

I know I screwed up. I also know I can probably convince her to stay, at least for a while. The problem is, she's been charmed by a lot of sweet-talkers over the years. It's going to take more than words to sort this mess out.

The car makes a turn and I hit the intercom. "Where are we going?"

"The office, sir. I seem to remember Harry Crane owes you a favor."

I blow out a sigh. "Thank you, Parker."

"You're welcome, sir."

Harry Crane is an ex-spook who became a PI when he retired. Parker's thinking more clearly than I am right now. If anyone can find Keeley, it's Crane.

There's very little traffic in the city at half past three in the morning, so we reach the Fox building in record time. I'm not really concentrating as I cross the lobby floor, but the expression on the face of the night guard catches my attention. He's holding a blanket in his hand and looks worried.

"Good evening, George." I nod to him. "You cold?"

He shakes his head. "No, sir. The fact is, we've got a bit of a...situation. I honestly didn't know how to handle it."

I'm torn. All I want to do is go and find Crane's number. He's got contacts all over. He's my best chance of finding Keeley.

But this is a problem in my building, involving my employees. I have a responsibility to them, too.

"What's going on, George?"

The man sighs, then gestures towards the bank of security cameras behind his desk. "It's probably better if I show you, sir."

"I know Mr. Servier was fired earlier this week, sir, so when I saw movement in his office…"

I have no idea what to expect when I lean over and follow his pointing finger to a screen. When it finally registers, though, I can't help smiling.

"I didn't know what to do, sir. I was about to take this up. Figured it might be a good idea." George lifts the blanket with a helpless look on his face.

"It's okay, George. You did well. Thank you. I'll handle this." I take the blanket from him, and he looks supremely grateful to be able to hand over the issue to someone else. I head for the elevator, making a mental note to give him a bonus.

The product manager I fired earlier in the week used to work out of a corner office on the fourteenth floor. I stand in the doorway and take a moment to look at the woman I've been chasing all over the city for the last four hours, while she sleeps on the couch. She looks tense, even in sleep, and when she shivers, I can't wait anymore. It's time to fix this.

Moving as quietly as possible, so as not to wake her, I wrap her in the blanket, then stand back and make a call. When it's done, I bend down and scoop her into my arms.

***

Keeley

I wake up gradually, warm and snuggled and feeling safe and relaxed. I don't really want to open my eyes, especially when I remember the way my life imploded last night. Staying on this couch in Servier's empty office sounds pretty good, at least for a little bit longer.

I had a dream, a lovely dream. I was flying, and Caden was right there with me. I wasn't alone. In the dream, I'd known I'd never be alone again. I'd really like to go back to it, and I snuggle down. Today's a Saturday. I can sleep a bit longer before I have to leave, and frankly, my dreamworld is a whole lot more inviting than the real one.

And then I hear a sound. It's too soft to be a vacuum cleaner, or the wind. I hear it a couple more times before I finally figure out what it is, and then there's no going back to sleep.

It's breathing.

Someone else is here, and I have a terrible feeling I know exactly who.

I crack open an eye, thinking the couch I fell asleep on feels very different now, but it's not until I see Caden's inky black hair that I have to admit I'm not on the couch. At least, not Servier's.

I'm curled up on Caden, who is in turn lying on his own, mile wide couch. In his penthouse. I'm wrapped in a soft, warm blanket which I definitely do not remember from last night, and my face flames. I hated having to go back to the Fox Building, but I had no other options, and I needed some breathing space, somewhere I could think

101

straight, work out what I was going to do next.

I'd completely failed to come up with any ideas, though, and had ended up crashing out in the vain hope that I'd be hit with some inspiration during the night, or at least after a few hours' sleep.

That Caden found me squatting in his most recently fired executive's office is just the cherry on the top of my complete humiliation.

I wriggle around, trying to figure out where my arms and legs are so that I can work out how to get off my gorgeous ex-bang buddy without waking him up. I've almost worked one arm free when his arms wrap around me like steel bars, making me yelp with surprise.

"You're not running out on me again, Keeley. At least, not without an explanation."

The grief I felt at losing him morphs into anger. It's easier to be angry at him now, here. I don't want to cry, and I don't want to look weak. But I do want to get away, and it looks like he's going to make that as hard as possible, which infuriates me. Why can't I ever leave a man on my terms? Why does it always have to be on theirs?

"You made it very clear last night that we're just temporary," I tell him, with as much dignity as I can muster while wrapped in a blanket over my slept-in cocktail dress, enclosed in his arms.

"Because I know I'm going to have to promote you," he says, calmly. "Much as you really are a brilliant assistant, you're too good for that. I want you to run one of the logistics divisions. I just haven't decided which one yet."

I crane my head back to meet his eyes, speechless with shock. "You what?"

"If you'd asked—"

"Don't give me that, Caden Fox!" I'm thoroughly pissed now, levering myself into a sitting position on his lap. "You could have told me that at any time, instead of going on about 'all good things have to end'. And what about the woman?"

He looks confused, and I want to slap him. "The blonde with legs like a racehorse? You got distracted with my orange juice in your hand?"

"Angela?"

"How the fuck should I know? She's your new girlfriend, not mine."

His arms tighten around me as I struggle to push away from him. "Angela DeMille runs Autistic Angels."

He pauses like that's supposed to mean something to me. I just glare at him, trying to ignore how his usually perfect hair has fallen into his beautiful eyes.

"It's the charity last night's event was in aid of. She was telling me they raised over a million dollars with the event, and I told her I'd match it. Naturally she was very pleased. She's also very happily married. To the city's first female mayor."

That takes the wind out of my sails. I manage to hold onto my anger and disbelief until he pulls out his phone and shows me a photo of the leggy Angela with an equally beautiful brunette, both in wedding dresses, looking ecstatic under a shower of confetti.

I drag my attention back to the thing that had broken me in the first place. "And 'all good things have to end'?"

He winces and has the grace to look ashamed.

"Look, I didn't even realize how I felt about you until last night. You were amazing. You weren't bored or boring. You shone, Keeley. You were a joy to have, to be seen with, and I was so proud to be the one escorting you. But, before you say anything, I know words are cheap. You've heard it all before, and it was always lies. I could tell you what a huge change, for the better, you've made in my life, but it would just be more words, and you've heard all that before. So, I decided to take action instead."

I eye him suspiciously. "What kind of action?"

He makes a move sideways, then straightens up again and strokes my hair off my face. I try not to press my face into his touch. I almost succeed. Almost.

"Are you going to make a break for the door as soon as I let go of you?"

I think about it for a moment, even though we both know it's a ridiculous question. His legs are far longer than mine. There's no way I could escape, and I'm not entirely sure I want to. I know that's the weak side of me talking, and I glare at him. "Move fast, Fox."

The ghost of a smile curves his lips, and then he leans down and lifts up a large box. "I'm hoping this will demonstrate how I feel about you in a way that you can believe."

I frown at the box. It's very plain, just a big cardboard box. "That's it?"

"Well, no," he says. "You have to open it."

I roll my eyes and reach up to pull the lid off the box before looking inside. My eyes widen, and I stare at the contents.

Straw, a couple of chew toys, a bowl of kibble, and one for water. And in the middle of it all, a scrap of fluff nuzzling through the straw before pouncing on one of the chew toys and trying to kill it.

It turns its face up towards me, and my heart just crumbles. "A puppy?"

I look up at him. "You got me a puppy?"

"No. I got *us* a puppy."

The air seems to have gone out of the room, because I can't take a full breath. My chest is too full, my heart expanding and flipflopping like an acrobat.

"But it's a big commitment," I murmur, unable to resist temptation any longer as I reach into the box to run my fingers over the puppy's fluffy body.

"It is a big commitment," he agrees. "But I want to make that commitment. Because I love you, and I only want you, forever."

He lifts his hand, and I gasp at the sight of the biggest, and most beautiful, diamond engagement ring I've ever seen in my life. One huge round diamond is surrounded by six more stones in the shape of a flower. "I'm ready to choose you, to commit to you, every day for the rest of my life, if you'll have me. Please, marry me."

I blink back tears of happiness before leaning around the box to kiss him, a gentle brush of lips which nonetheless has heat slithering in my belly. "I love you, too. Yes. Please."

He slides the ring onto my finger and kisses me as deeply as the box between us will allow.

"Now, there is another matter to attend to. You scared the crap out of me last night," he says, setting the box aside. "I've had plenty of time to think of an appropriate punishment, and I think now is a good time to administer it."

He stands with me in his arms, and carries me towards his bedroom, and I wriggle around in his arms to murmur in his ear. "You mean you've actually chosen a single punishment?"

He pretends to glare at me. "You're going to find out, slowly, sweetly, and screaming my name."

I shiver in his arms, wet heat already gathering between my thighs. "Sounds perfect."

THE END

Read on for a sneak peek of *Max*, the second book in the Her Dominant Boss series!

Max: Her Dominant Boss #2

Shay

I clutch my glass of lukewarm champagne as Harry Hennessy takes the stage. Around me, the employees of Hennessy's Hotel and Conference Center fall silent. We may pretend to be here for the champagne and free buffet, but that's not the real reason.

Well, it's not mine.

Hennessy throws two big parties a year, one in the summer and one at Christmas. It's the beginning of June, schools are out, and we're all gathered on the rooftop terrace at the Carnegie Ridge Park Hotel, ostensibly enjoying the free food and drink.

I've barely eaten anything and the half glass of champagne I knocked back about twenty minutes ago for Dutch courage is already warming my blood. This is it, the moment I've been waiting for, the moment I got a little drunk trying to prepare for. I'm about to finally, *finally*, get the job I really want, the job I've been working towards since graduating high school.

Hennessy looks around and smiles, keen to make us wait, to draw out the tension until someone starts crying. Okay, that would be me. Because I've applied for the Events Coordinator job three times now. They say the third time's the charm, right? I've worked for Hennessy since graduating high school. I know the venue like the insides of my own eyelids. Six years I've worked here, and when the Events Coordinator job first opened up, four years ago, I went for it, only to discover that two years of experience on the job didn't qualify me. So two years ago, when it opened up again, I applied again.

Still not enough experience.

It's been six years. I've been here longer than every other applicant, most of whom applied straight out of college. I've put in immensely long hours and never asked for a raise. I've taken on every challenge that's ever been thrown at me, well, at my manager who then usually passed it down to me, and I triumphed every time. I've got the experience, the client relation skills, and relationships with every vendor in the city who provides products and services for Hennessy events. This job is mine.

Mine.

"I know you're all keen to know who our new Events Coordinator will be, since Mitchell Haynes is now moving on to bigger and better things. So, without further ado, it gives me great pleasure to announce, the new Events Coordinator is…"

Hennessy's eyes land on me and skate away before I can smile in response. Something settles in my belly, cold and hard, and I push the sensation away. This is it. My dream job. Right in the palm of my han—

"Kelley Riker."

I stare at him, then at Kelley's perfect chestnut curls as she bounces up to the stage to shake Hennessy's hand. She turns and smiles at us all, and I want to vomit. She's the same age as me and has been working here for about six months, having bounced around a bit after, as she put it, 'drinking and napping' her way through college. She can't remember anything but never writes anything down. I've ended up doing most of her work as well as mine.

What the *fuck*?

Hennessy steps down off the stage, and I shoulder my way through the crowd to plant myself squarely in front of him. I'm a larger girl, so I'm hard to ignore, but he does his best. Right up to the moment where I lose my patience and grab his arm.

"Mr. Hennessy," I manage to grind out between my teeth, then dial back my temper. I can't yell at my boss. As frustrated as I am in my job, constantly picking up for people who know way less than I do, I do need a job. And I'm good at this one. I just wish someone would actually reward me for that. "Mr. Hennessy, what makes Kelley more qualified than me for the Events Coordinator position?"

He has the grace to look embarrassed, as well he might, since he all but told me the job was mine when I interviewed for it. "I'm really sorry, Shay. I know how much this job would have meant to you, but the fact is, she has a college degree."

I stare at him, my jaw on the floor. "Six years of experience doesn't count for anything?"

"Of course it does, Shay, don't be ridiculous. But I discussed it with the board, and we agreed that college prepares workers for management in a way that experience in lower level positions simply doesn't. I'm very sorry, but that's the policy now."

Spoken like a man who went to college. I blink back the tears, only too aware of what he's saying, what this means for me. I'll never rise above Events Assistant, no matter how much experience I get. And it doesn't matter that six years ago, I was all set to go to Yale.

All that matters to the board is that I didn't go. I didn't graduate. I didn't get a piece of paper which is apparently worth more than all my experience put together. Fury coils in my belly as I realize, once again, my future has been stolen by a man in an expensive suit. Only in this case, I work for the asshole in question.

My jaw tightens. I will not cry in front of this man who thinks I'm some kind of lower class citizen just because I didn't go to college. I won't.

I'll wait until I'm alone in the elevator, like any self-respecting woman.

Of course, standing in the elevator, hot tears running down my face, the door pings open just a few floors down. I scrub my face dry, losing my grip on my purse and sending it crashing to the floor just as the most beautiful man I've ever seen steps inside, wearing a very expensive suit.

***

Max

I do my best to ignore the curvy blonde currently pretending she hasn't just been crying her eyes out as she picks up her things. I can't hold up the pretence for long, though, and I stoop and hand her a dark blue pen which looks as if it's made of glass, then stand and move away. She clearly doesn't want any attention, although I would imagine she's used to receiving it. Even in the hideous skirt suit she's wearing, her body is spectacular enough to turn a man's head at forty paces.

I also didn't miss the way her lip curled when she registered my Kiton suit. I should be glad she's not interested in a man with money, but with a surname instantly recognizable around the world, I'm more intrigued than anything. A woman who doesn't find billionaires attractive? Why aren't there more of those in this city?

I shake my head and force myself to focus on the huge problem my mother just dumped in my lap. Which is actually unfair of me, because it's entirely my fault. If I hadn't been so busy trying to avoid the attentions of my last assistant, I might have realized she wasn't doing the work she was being paid to do. Namely, organize the annual Deakin Family Foundation Midsummer Gala.

Now the gala is three weeks away, and all we have is a venue, and that's only because the foundation has been holding its parties at the same place for over twenty years, so the date is permanently booked. However, nothing else is in place. No vendors, no caterers, *nothing*.

My mother is not pleased.

"I'm not saying you're to blame, Maximilian, but she was your assistant, and I had expected you to take more interest in the organization of this year's gala anyway. Instead, you handed the job off to some floozy who was more interested in landing a rich husband than organizing our biggest fundraising event. I don't need to tell you what the consequences will be if this event doesn't go ahead."

Her words ring in my ears even as the hum of the elevator rises around us. I suddenly realize the mechanical whine has risen to an uncomfortable pitch, but there's no time to question it before there's a crunch and the elevator jerks to a halt. In the same moment, the lights blink out, plunging us into darkness.

"What. The. *Fuck*?"

I smile, even as my cock twitches at the sound of her voice, strong and musical. "Relax," I tell her. "It's probably just a power glitch. The lights will come on again in a second."

Several seconds pass, and I swear I can feel her glaring at me.

"You were saying?"

She swallows, loud enough for me to hear it where I'm standing several feet away, and I realize she's scared. Doing her best to control it, which is admirable, particularly as most women of my acquaintance would be screaming blue murder by now, but still scared.

"Here," I say, "walk towards me."

"Why?"

I've rarely heard a more suspicious tone directed my way. Well, not since I stopped playing pranks on my brothers as a child. Mother would be proud. Forcing myself to repress a sigh, I hold out my hand, then remember she can't see it, which is the problem. God, Deakin, get a grip.

"Because if you're scared of the dark, or small spaces, or both, you can hold my hand, and it will help."

There follows a long silence, then I hear her move. Fabric brushes against my fingertips, but my hand closes on nothing. Instead, I hear her pressing buttons, and I smile. Smart girl. She's bypassed the comfort portion of the evening and has moved straight into problem-solving, in spite of her fear. I'm impressed.

I'm also a little surprised at how disappointed I am. I hadn't realized until this moment how much I was looking forward to experiencing the texture of her skin.

And now my brain has gone somewhere entirely inappropriate, and I'm damn glad it's dark in here.

"Hello, can you hear me?" A disembodied voice addresses us.

"Yes! I mean, yes," she says, lowering her tone from its initial shriek. "The elevator just stopped, and the lights have gone out."

"Okay, I'm really sorry about that. There was some issue with the power, but the lights should have come on again by now. We're checking the emergency generator now. How many of you are in there?"

"Two."

"Any medical issues we should know about?"

"Well it wouldn't do you much good if there were, would it?" she mutters quietly, making me chuckle. Raising her voice, she responds, "No, we're fine."

"Okay. Give us a minute to get the lights back on. I'm waiting on an ETA from the fire department."

"Okay."

Her voice trembles, and this time I can't help myself. I move towards her, and my hand finds her arm. She gasps, then reluctantly reaches for me, her hands brushing down my chest until she suddenly snatches them back. "I'm sorry."

"Don't be. I was enjoying that."

She makes a disgusted sound and goes to pull away, but I keep a firm grip of her arm. Okay, it was an asshole thing to say. I was hoping to lighten the situation with humor. Clearly, that was the wrong way to go.

Still, she may be too proud to want to take comfort from a stranger, but that doesn't mean I won't do what's right. I slide my hand down to hers, then interlock our fingers. There's a click, and suddenly the lights come on. The look on her face is a gift, such relief, and it makes something tighten in my gut. I don't want her to be sad or scared, but I'm not going to think too closely about why. She's not mine to take care of.

Not yet, anyway.

The radio crackles and the tinny voice makes her jump. I rub my thumb over her palm to calm her, and she stares at her hand, then at my face. Her eyes are a luminous green, and I find myself falling into them. She seems just as intent on my face as I am on hers, so that we both miss what's being said by the emergency technician.

"I'm sorry." I suddenly realize someone asked a question. "What was that?"

"I said, it's going to be about an hour before the fire department can get here. Are you guys going to be okay?"

"Yes," I say, without thinking, then I look at her face. The click of the radio going dead emphasizes the lost look in her eyes, and her lips tremble. She looks like she's about to burst into tears, and I can only think of one thing to do about it, which is cover her mouth with mine.

I only meant to distract her, but the moment my lips touch hers, all conscious thought evaporates. Soft and warm and pliant. At first she freezes, but then her mouth opens on a moan, and I need no second invitation. I groan, plunging my tongue into the hot, sweet, welcoming cavern of her mouth, sliding my hands into her hair and tilting her head to give me greater access.

I pull back. She stares at me, confusion filling her eyes. As much as I want to drown myself in her, though, there's one thing I have to know first.

"Yes?" I ask.

She frowns. "Yes, what?"

"Do you want this?" I ask her. I'm a thousand per cent sure she's with me right now, but a gentleman never makes assumptions about such things, and my mother raised me to be a gentleman.

I see the moment where she struggles with her conscience. After all, we're strangers, although not for much longer, if I have anything to say about it.

"Fuck it," she says. "Yes."

Order now on Amazon!

ABOUT THE AUTHOR

K.R. Max loves ice cream, big fluffy dogs, and stories where the woman finds her place with a super-hot guy who adores her. She specializes in dominant heroes and the sweet, innocent women who bring them to their knees!

If you like a fast read with a guaranteed happy ever after, lots of super-hot and VERY dirty shenanigans, and NO cheating OR cliffhangers, K. R. Max is for you!

You can find her on Facebook, at
http://www.facebook.com/krmaxwrites/

You can also sign up for her mailing list at
http://eepurl.com/cOtnGz

Made in the USA
Las Vegas, NV
29 March 2022

46495614R00073